D0443440

insight

insight

A Novel

Diana Greenwood

ZONDERVAN®

ZONDERVAN.com/
AUTHORTRACKER
follow your favorite authors

We want to hear from you. Please send your comments about this book to us in care of zreview@zondervan.com. Thank you.

ZONDERVAN

Insight
Copyright © 2011 by Diana Greenwood

This title is also available as a Zondervan ebook.
Visit www.zondervan.com/ebooks.

Requests for information should be addressed to:

Zondervan, *Grand Rapids, Michigan 49530*

ISBN 978-0-310-72314-1

Cover design: Jeff Gifford
Cover photography: iStockphoto
Interior design: Sherri Hoffman

Printed in the United States of America

11 12 13 14 15 /DCI/ 23 22 21 20 19 18 17 16 15 14 13 12 11 10 9 8 7 6 5 4 3 2 1

insight

Chapter 1

It wasn't a scream, exactly, coming from behind the closed door of my mother's bedroom. It was more of a moan that started small and rose in pitch to a sharp yip as if a dog were dreaming and someone snuck up and gave it a swift kick. I would never kick a dog. But there were days I wished I could kick my mother, and with all that noise, today was one of them.

Her next yell was loud, but everything is loud when you live way out in the middle of nowhere like we did. Even crows scared themselves, the air was so quiet.

Just that morning Grandma said, "Only a fool would live five miles from town with no way to move around come winter. Even a town as puny as Portage is better than nothing if you live close in."

I guess we were fools, then, or my mother was. She picked this place. "Far enough from town for privacy and

far enough from the Wisconsin River and the canals to con-
fuse the mosquitoes," she pointed out to back up her decision. But the real reason was my mother liked to keep an eye
on my father. She figured living out here would keep him
home. She was wrong. Now Grandma lived with us in our
tiny house, and she took up more space than he ever did.

Grandma still looked pretty young, no gray hair and
hardly any wrinkles. Having had her only child at the ripe
age of eighteen, she was done with that early. Unlike my
mother, birthing her second right now at the age of thirty-
eight, ten years after I was born.

To prove we were all alone, Grandma'd haul me out
back when the switchgrass was dry, stand overlooking the
rocky dell, and scream "Fire!" as loud as she could. We'd
hear "Fire, fire, fire," growing fainter and fainter. She'd
wait a bit as if someone would rush right up to save us.

Then she'd say, "See? Not a soul within earshot."

Sometimes she'd shout my name to the sky, calling
"Elvira!" at the top of her lungs, and she'd say it bounced
off the clouds with nowhere else to go and came right back
to stick in her throat. She'd clear her throat to get my name
out and even that echoed.

But Grandma's shouts were nothing compared to the
noise of having a baby, and my mother's next yell was
much louder than her last. While she suffered behind her
door, my job was to keep the washtub filled so Grandma
could keep everything clean. My mother was birthing that
baby without the midwife, as she couldn't get here, and
it was too late now to try to get to town with snow to the
eaves and no man to shovel us out.

I lugged the kettle from the sink to our old Wedgewood

stove. The blue flame puffed and sputtered. Out of habit, I glanced at the stove's little round clock as I did every winter morning, usually while I ate alone, making mountains out of oatmeal with my spoon and squinting in the dim light of the kitchen to read our only cookbook. While I waited for the water to heat, my eyes traveled to where the book lay on the counter. It was a collection of recipes from the Lutheran Ladies' Guild, bound and hand typed, with a cover of red gingham pasted on and fraying at the corners. It was already well used when we picked it up for a dime at the annual St. John's rummage sale, and I'd added a few stains to the pages. When we paid, a white-haired church lady in a sky-blue sweater had grasped my mother's hand and said, "Peace be with you." My mother took a step back. We weren't used to people being nice to us. But the lady smiled and handed the cookbook to me, so I felt as if it were mine.

The dessert section was my favorite. I'd imagine making all those fancy cakes and complicated desserts like éclairs, so foreign-sounding and pretty, thick with whipped cream in a flaky crust, chocolate syrup drizzled on top. I'd read so many recipes I'd lose track of time, the ticking of the stove clock finally sinking into my brain, reminding me it was time to leave. Then I'd start my miss-the-bus worrying. But every day, a part of me wished I could skip school altogether, go back to bed where it was warm, and spend the morning reading recipes.

Except it wasn't morning and school was cancelled, winter vacation extended because of the worst blizzard on record. If I were a baby, I wouldn't have picked today to show up. Before the signal was lost, the radio said thirteen below and dropping. It was already pitch black and it was only five o'clock. Howling wind circled the house, rattling the windows, and an icy draft sneaked under the back door. I stuffed a dishcloth in the crack. The ceiling light flickered. I got candles out and set a box of wooden matchsticks on the kitchen table in case we lost electricity. I imagined the only thing worse than having a baby in the first place would be having a baby in the dark.

Thumbtacked to the wall was our complimentary calendar from Jensen's Hardware, all the days crossed out leading up to today. January 10th, 1943. The words "Happy New Year" on the calendar in fancy red and blue letters looked hopeful, as though words alone could change my mood. But the words didn't lift my spirits. I couldn't think of one thing happy about starting another year. On the other hand, it couldn't be worse than the one we'd just left behind.

The kettle whistled. I sniffed because the kitchen smelled like scorched toast from crumbs caught under the burner and I was afraid they'd catch fire. We kept a box of Arm & Hammer Baking Soda on a shelf beside the stove for emergencies. As I reached to grab the kettle, steam bit my wrist and left a red streak. Maybe it wasn't fire I needed to fear but water instead. The *Lutheran Ladies' Guild Cookbook* had a Household Tips section and I'd practically memorized it. A baking soda paste would soothe the sting and stop a blister. But I didn't have time to make it.

I heard another snap of a yell. It was exactly the kind of yell my mother used when I broke her last china serving bowl — a terrible, end-of-the-world yell. I wondered if Grandma had broken something too, but then she poked her head out and shrieked, "Elvira Witsil, get that water in here. This baby's coming foot first."

She slammed the door in my face, forcing me to put the big iron kettle down on the oak-plank floor, sloshing a few scalding drops that spread and stained and looked like beads of blood in the red glow from the last of the coals in the fireplace. I'd have to get more wood next.

Behind the door, Grandma said in her fed-up tone, "Trust you to have a baby backwards, Connie. It's going to be long and hard."

I went in, trying not to look at my mother, who was acting feverish. Her wavy brown hair, usually in a braid like mine, was all matted with sweat, her face was purple, and there was a lot of mess I didn't want to see between her legs where that baby was trying to get out. I saw the foot, though, blue as a bruise, with Grandma's hand around it about to give a pull.

"Don't stand there with your mouth hanging open like you're trapping flies," Grandma said. "Pour that water in the tub."

"I am," I said, but the kettle was heavy and my arms shook. Steaming water slopped over the edge of the wash-tub, splashing my feet and burning like a bee sting right through my wool socks. At this rate, I was going to need a baking soda *bath* to treat my burns.

"Now look what you've done, Elvira! Go get the mop and sop that up. And get some more wood. This baby'll die before it takes its first breath, it's so cold in here."

My mother sat up like she was a puppet and someone had just yanked her strings. "Will you stop talking?" she screamed. "God, oh, God, I can't bear this pain!"

"Fat lot of good God's going to do you," said Grandma. "Where was he when you got yourself into this?"

My mother scrunched up her face so hard her eyes were puffy lines and her cheeks big as a chipmunk's, and her long hair fell forward and covered her bare chest. I was glad, because it embarrassed me she had no clothes on. I never wanted to see my mother like that, naked and bloody, and I swore then and there if that's how you had to look to have a baby I'd never have one as long as I lived. I didn't realize I'd said it out loud until Grandma, who hardly ever laughed, laughed about that.

Grandma was pretty mad at my mother for having this baby, and she continued to make her opinions known. She said my mother was a fool for having a child so late. She said WWII was started by one evil man with nothing better to do than sit around figuring out ways to get people killed. She thought raising children alone, now that my father was missing in action, gone before my mother even knew she was pregnant, was downright idiotic.

My father's ship blew up the first week he was out — not bombed or anything, just due to some kind of engine failure — in the middle of the night when all the crew was sleeping. They never found the bodies. "Must have been a mess," Grandma'd said a hundred times, "and doesn't it just figure that good-for-nothing would go out in a flash without doing anything to get the glory."

My mother always yelled back, "How could I have known my husband would go missing and I'd be stuck in this god-forsaken place, pregnant, with a self-centered daughter, a grouchy old woman, and not a penny to my name?"

But the yelling my mother was doing right now hurt

my ears. I clicked the door shut, filled the kettle, and put it back on to boil. The wind was a high-pitched whine, as if it were a poor lost thing looking for a place to settle. I shivered, the mudroom icy as I grabbed a stack of wood for the fireplace. My father's old boots were by the back door. No one had noticed when I placed them side by side, laced and polished and buffed the way he liked them. My mother was right. I *was* a self-centered daughter. My father was missing because of me. No Lutheran Ladies' remedy would soothe that ache. It burned from the inside out.

It didn't seem real, my father gone for good, especially when he'd been gone so many times before. But he came back those other times. He'd be a little worse for wear, maybe a bruise or two turning yellow around his eyes, but my mother always let him back in. The house would be silent, the air thick and crackling with too many nerves on edge, until his smile would finally break my mother's will.

My father was unpredictable. You never knew what he might do. I liked that best about him and I missed it most. But my mother needed him to come home on time from a regular job and stuff dollar bills in the savings jar behind the bread box. She needed him to fix the step on the back porch and stop disappearing for days on end. She needed him to pour his own whiskey down the kitchen sink so she wouldn't have to.

With him gone for good, my mother was a fire ready to light but missing a match. Grandma'd stepped right in and taken over. We watched my mother's stomach grow and grow and worked ourselves into a routine of eat, chores, sleep, eat, chores, sleep, with arguments for entertainment. Then my sister struggled out and all that changed.

Chapter 2

My mother gave my sister a name that didn't suit her: Jessamyn Rayann, after my father's mother and his first name, Ray. Grandma refused to acknowledge the association to my father's family, so she called her Jessie instead. I had to agree the nickname was better.

Jessie was strange from the start. Being born left foot first in the dead of winter must have done it. She cried all the time and those cries echoed more than all the other sounds combined. Drove me crazy those first few months. I stuffed cotton batting into my ears. Shut myself in my bedroom closet and pulled a blanket over my head, just to get away from that sound. For some reason, my mother didn't seem to mind. She coddled Jessie as though she were the first baby she'd ever seen, and the prettiest too. She cooed and played patty-cake and tested the temperature of Jessie's precious infant formula on her wrist, frowning if it seemed the slightest bit too warm. Formula was rationed, and of course buying it meant we went without something else. Like real milk from cows, for instance. I'd never craved milk until we couldn't have it.

My mother played "This Little Piggy" over and over, and I had no memory of her ever playing that with me. But Jessie cried anyway — deep, chesty sobs, as if the world was too big or too loud or too bright for her — no matter what my mother did. Grandma took to taking long walks in the woods, and I'd never been so happy to go to school in my life.

But by the time Jessie was a year old she'd settled into silence, and I found myself coaxing her to talk. "Say, El-vir-a," I said, drawing out the syllables. "Come on, you can do it." I wanted to be first. I wanted her to say my name before she said *Mama*, the word my mother expected for weeks. But Jessie stared at me, all green eyes under a mop of unruly brown curls, and did a funny kind of hum, air in and out through puckered lips. No words.

The second she learned to walk, Jessie stuck to me like glue. I'd be dusting or sweeping, lost in my thoughts, and there she'd be as if she appeared out of thin air, right under my feet, just asking to be stepped on. I could never even go to the bathroom by myself without Jessie banging the door open and coming in to pester me. She'd plant herself in one spot and lift her arms, flexing her fingers open, closed, open, closed, which meant *pick me up*. Five seconds later, she'd lean over and point to the ground, which meant *put me down*. My mother would hold out her arms but Jessie always toddled right back to me, grabbed a fistful of my overalls about knee-level, and hung on.

I made Jessie a little rag doll out of scraps from Grandma's sewing basket so she'd have something to do besides trail my steps. "Let's name your doll," I said, making the doll dance on the arm of the sofa. "How about Betsy? Do you like that name?" No answer, of course. Jessie hummed a tuneless ditty but wouldn't say a word. "How about Jane? She looks like a Jane. She has nice blue-button eyes."

Actually, the doll looked more like a Mabel who needed the beauty parlor. I'd had trouble attaching the yarn hair, and it stuck up every which way in orange spirals. Grandma had helped embroider the mouth, but she'd made the lips pursed as though the doll had sucked something sour. Jessie liked Mabel, though, I could tell. She carried her everywhere. But Mabel didn't stop Jessie trailing me, and Mabel couldn't make Jessie talk any more than I could.

By the time Jessie was almost two and she'd still done nothing but grunt and point, dragging Mabel around but not calling her by name, my mother started to worry. Her precious, perfect baby wasn't so perfect after all.

"Jessie should be talking by now," she said about fifty times a day.

"She's an unusual child, to put it mildly," Grandma said. "Most children chatter a mile a minute by the time they're her age. She probably can talk and was just born disobedient. Like that fool you married. Ask him to do one thing and he'd do the opposite."

My mother ignored that comment.

"Something's wrong with her," she said, twisting the tail of her braid around a finger. "I can feel it. What two-year-old stands at a window all day long? From the second Elvira leaves to catch the school bus until she sees her coming up the drive, Jessie doesn't move, doesn't play, doesn't utter a sound. It's odd, I tell you."

My mother already had plenty to worry about, living off the war checks, never near enough, and the savings jar was almost empty. But I didn't feel sorry for her. She'd been blind to me since Jessie was born. And with Christmas only two weeks away, I had my hopes up for Holiday Cake. For days, the *Lutheran Ladies' Guild Cookbook* lay on the kitchen counter where I'd left it, open to the recipe and marked with a slip of ribbon. I hoped she'd notice and send me to the market in town for ingredients. I'd stand in line two hours for butter if I had to, since butter was rationed and hard to get. That Holiday Cake was the least I deserved.

My twelfth birthday had passed with barely a nod, given all the fuss about Jessie not talking. I didn't blame Jessie. I wanted to. But Jessie couldn't bake a cake or buy me a present. I'd been wishing for a new book. Something good to read besides the cookbook and the Bobbsey Twins I'd outgrown three years before. Twelve-year-olds needed a book like *A Tree Grows in Brooklyn*, a modern book; the one Mrs. Keller, the Portage librarian, said I'd love. Even the title filled my mind with possibilities. Mrs. Keller understood that I was beyond baby books. She was a librarian and librarians were better than mothers at that sort of thing.

I'd casually mentioned *A Tree Grows in Brooklyn* during supper when everyone's mouths were full of mashed potatoes. Grandma said, not even bothering to swallow first, "I forbid that book in this house. There are passages inappropriate for twelve-year-old ears." How she knew that was beyond me, and of course that only made me want to read it even more. But then she said, "Elvira, you best heed my words or you won't set foot in that library again."

So I shut up about that book. But I didn't stop thinking about it. If my father were here, he would have found a way to get it for me. It would have been our secret. I pictured him winking, heading for the back door, and pointing to the corners of the book poking out from under his shirt. He would've grabbed his parka off the hook, jumped the back steps before my mother could stop him, and headed to our favorite rock where we always hid from my mother when she was in one of her moods. He would have known I'd follow, stepping in the tracks his boots made in the snow.

But nobody got me a present that year. My mother should have. And Grandma should've remembered even if a hand-me-down pair of gloves or one of her knitted scarves was all I got. So I was resentful when my mother announced we'd be taking Jessie to see the doctor in town.

"How will we pay?" I asked, tasting Holiday Cake in my memories and imagining the feel of new paper in that book I didn't get.

My mother fumed. When she was mad, she stomped and was likely to pick up something to throw. I edged toward the back door.

"You saying I don't take good enough care of you, Miss Elvira, Queen of Sheba?" she said. "How can you be so self-ish when your sister might be deaf or mute or sick? Your twelve-year-old mouth needs to stop its whining."

At least she remembered I'd turned twelve. "I'm not whining," I said. "I'm just wondering where we'd find money for the doctor since we don't even have enough to buy cranberries and walnuts for Holiday Cake. You used to always make Holiday Cake."

"Elvira, I don't have the wherewithal or the mind for a celebration this year. Christmas can come and go for all I care. Quit wishing for what you can't have. You're a dreamer."

Grandma stuck her nose in like no one was allowed to be mad but her.

"Just like her father was," she said. "Connie, you leave that girl alone. It's not her fault you're in this pickle."

Grandma always found a way to get in a word or two about my mother's inability to make a solid decision. I was glad she was sticking up for me, even though it wouldn't last.

But Jessie wasn't deaf or mute or sick. She was faking; I just knew it.

☙

It took us a long time to get ready. Even though the snow was light, it was bitter cold. The kind of cold that makes your nose run just thinking about it. I pulled on woolens, overalls, thick socks, and my mother's old coat that hung almost to my ankles. I wrapped a knitted muffler twice around my neck.

My mother wore my father's old brown parka, which had a hood lined with rabbit fur. Although he'd been gone over two years now, I could still picture my father wearing it. On him the parka had looked right, proper, like beige and a badge on the Columbia County sheriff. I used to notice how green his eyes were when the hood was up. Once, when I was small, he'd zipped me inside to keep me warm. I'd wrapped my legs around him tight to keep from slipping, since he'd had a bounce in his step that day. His breath as he whistled came out in little puffs of white air. I'd felt safe inside that parka.

But my mother looked wrong in it, like a mean brown bear standing next to us as I zipped Jessie up. I thought if my mother were a real bear, she'd swallow my sister whole, she was so little.

Grandma, ready first, was impatient to go now the decision had been made.

"Hurry up, for pity's sake," she said. "Before we all faint from overheating."

We had to walk a mile before we even hit US 51, right where the bus picked me up for school, and when we did finally get there, my fingers were stiff. Wet breath made little blobs of ice on my muffler. My mother looked up and down the frozen highway, holding Jessie's hand, resigned to the wait. I wished she'd hold my hand too.

Since Jessie'd been born, I'd felt invisible. Not like I was ever the center of attention, but if I didn't make myself useful, no one even noticed I lived and breathed. No one ever asked *how was school* or *did you make a friend today* or *your forehead is hot, maybe you have a fever.* In the Bobbsey Twins books, the mother always asked those things. Were there really mothers like that? No one ever checked to see if my toes were squished in my worn-out school shoes and maybe I needed new ones before my feet stuck in that squished shape and I'd walk pigeon-toed forever. I carried anger at my mother for questions never asked and my hand never held.

A green panel truck appeared in the distance, headlamps on. My mother stuck her thumb out. Jessie copied her. She looked stupid standing there, a two-year-old hitch-hiking. What would it be like to hitchhike my way out of Portage? Go to Madison and see the big city. Get a job in a library shelving books. The orderly shelves. The tidy card files. The smell of lemon polish on the old wooden reading tables and the musty tang of books. I could sleep in a cot in the basement. Get a hot plate and heat up Campbell's tomato soup for supper. I wouldn't need much. Maybe work my way up to librarian and be just like Mrs. Keller, helping girls pick books when their miserable mothers wouldn't.

The panel truck passed us up. I practically froze solid before a blue DeSoto stopped and gave us a ride almost all the way into town, dropping us where US 51 turned into New Pinery Road.

The doctor's office was actually the front rooms of a white farmhouse on Maple Street in a regular neighbor-hood where fathers kept the sidewalks shoveled. Some houses had evergreen wreaths on the doors. It was cold but clear and sunny, so drapes had been swept aside. You could see right into the neat living rooms, and cheerful Christmas trees with cranberry strings, tinsel, and shiny ornaments were visible in the picture windows.

Somebody was baking. The smell of cinnamon rose on the crisp winter air, and I tugged at my muffler to get a better whiff. My mouth watered for Holiday Cake, loaded with cinnamon and cranberries and walnuts. If I could just get enough cranberries, I could leave the walnuts out of the recipe to save money. Keep a few cranberries to string for a tree. Maybe I'd cut blue spruce branches and make a wreath for our door too. Or maybe I wouldn't. Nobody else cared, why should I?

The doctor didn't have a wreath. Maybe he didn't celebrate Christmas, like Rachael Perlman in my class. Rachael's mother sent a note to excuse her from our Christmas card project. Our teacher made Rachael clean out the art cupboards instead. Seemed like punishment, organizing all the scraps of construction paper into one box, washing paintbrushes in the sink at the back of the room, and peeling the paste off lids so the tubs would close properly. Didn't seem fair. I couldn't remember what the name of Rachael's holiday was, but surely there were cards for it. At milk break Rachael leaned on the chain-link fence, tracing the wire diamonds with a gloved finger, her back to the icy playground swarming with kids. I thought about walking right up and telling her I didn't care if her holiday was different; I'd be her friend. I thought about saying, *I know what it's like to be ignored.* But I couldn't drum up the nerve and she'd never paid any attention to me in the past, so what was the point?

We stomped on the doctor's porch and a bell clanged when Grandma opened the front door. Inside, it was overly warm. We dripped on the floor and stood in puddles, our coats heaped on wooden benches. The room smelled damp and stale like a root cellar filled with potatoes. We waited a long time to be called.

The doctor stuck instruments down Jessie's throat, looked in there with a light on a stick, knocked on her back, and listened to her chest with a stethoscope. He felt under her ears. Walked behind her and clapped his hands. Jessie smiled but didn't turn around.

Grandma saw that smile and voiced her own conclusions about Jessie. "She's stubborn," she said. "Stubborn as a mule on a rainy day. She hears fine."

My mother glared, picking at the white paper on the doctor's table, smoothing it, picking it, smoothing it. "What do you think it is?" she asked the doctor.

He frowned, rubbed his chin, and then folded his arms, the sleeves of his doctor's coat rolled up to show hairy wrists and a silver watch.

"She's never said anything?" he asked.

My mother shook her head.

"She hums when she follows me around," I said, and everybody looked at me. I felt my face go hot. But I kept going. "Well, she does. I'm the only one who ever hears her, because she never leaves me alone. She hums all the time."

The doctor nodded. "She's stubborn," he said, looking at Grandma, returning her satisfied smile. "Everything God gave her seems to work. Nothing's wrong I can find. Let her be. She'll talk when she's ready."

Grandma paid, scowling while she handed over five silver dollars, picking them out of her black coin purse one by one as if it pained her to part with them. Which I suppose it did. She and my mother thumped out, leaving me to gather Jessie's pile of clothes and get her dressed.

I tugged her sweater over her curls, static electricity sending the spirals every which way. Jessie squirmed, her woolens bagging at the knees as I grabbed her snow pants. Jessie stared at me, her brows raised in a curious expression. Her mouth curled in an impish smile like the fifty-cent Kewpie dolls at the corner Rexall on Cook and DeWitt. Then she stared at the white linoleum where a little yellow puddle formed, a trickle flowing down her leg and over her sock. It figured. The elastic was worn out in every pair of rubber pants that Jessie owned, and there was no money to buy any new ones. I wiped up the puddle with a wad of the doctor's tissues and pushed them down to the bottom of a metal garbage can. I'd brought an extra diaper. Since school was out for winter vacation, my mother had shoved the changing-Jessie chore off on me. Refusing would only invite another lecture.

The cloth diaper still smelled faintly of bleach as I pulled it from my pocket, folded the white square into a triangle, and plopped Jessie back up on the doctor's table. I yanked off her damp socks, woolens, and the stretched-out rubber pants, then pinned the fresh diaper, not caring if I stuck her and drew blood. Jessie didn't struggle, not even when I tugged the wet socks back over her toes, which were so ticklish she usually couldn't stand me touching them. I zipped up her snow pants and laced her boots. She lay unmoving on the examination table, staring blankly up at me the whole time as if she'd died with her eyes open.

The door squeaked on its hinges and Grandma stuck her head in. "Elvira, what are you waiting for, the first thaw? Get a move on." She shut the door so hard my teeth rattled. Jessie didn't even blink.

I stuffed the dirty diaper into the doctor's garbage can too. I knew it was wasteful but I wasn't walking home with that in my pocket. Jessie flopped over my shoulder as I picked her up, her body limp and heavy.

For a second, I wanted to pinch her.

For a second, I wished she'd never been born.

Chapter 3

Jessie was finished with diapers after the day at the doctor's. None of us really knew why, but I had the sneaking suspicion Jessie wanted to spare me the chore of changing her. I felt guilty about that and dangled freshly bleached cloth diapers in front of her. Smiled even, as though I didn't mind one bit. She just shook her head at diapers and strutted off to the bathroom, scooted up onto the seat, and did her business.

But Jessie wasn't ready to talk until one bright June day, six months after she turned four years old, and when she did speak it was not a regular word like other kids might say. It was a cuss word. Not one Grandma or my mother ever used either.

Jessie said "damnation" with the emphasis on the *nation*, like a preacher scolding his congregation for sinning all week. She marched around the house saying it, as though enjoying the stunned expressions on our faces.

Grandma shook her head, appalled. "She's the spitting image of that traveling fire-and-brimstone fanatic the sheriff ran out of town a few years back. But she wasn't even born then. Where'd she hear that word?"

I didn't know. Neither did my mother. Nobody in my house went to church, let alone believed in traveling fire-and-brimstone fanatics. The only churchy things I'd ever seen around here were the doilies that covered the rips in the upholstery on the arms of our overstuffed chair. Grandma said Catholic ladies wore doilies on their heads. That must look silly. I did remember one Sunday; the only radio program that came in clear was a sermon, the minister's voice sharp and mean sounding, with gloomy organ music playing in the background. "Repent," he roared over the radio waves, "or you'll burn in the depths of the earth." When I asked Grandma what that meant, she said it was a personal message for disrespectful children.

But I didn't remember any cussing before my mother turned off the radio program, and that program was before Jessie was born too. Even though we'd waited so long for her to talk, after a few hours of Jessie *not* saying damnation, we breathed a sigh of relief and thought it was over. A fluke.

My mother told Jessie to wash up for supper. Forks clinked as I set the table, and I heard water running in the bathroom.

"Jessie," I called. "Come on. Supper's ready."

When she didn't come I went to find her. The *Amos 'n' Andy Show* was on WMAQ out of Chicago, and for once the signal was good. I hated to miss one second of it. I planned on dragging Jessie back by the ear if I had to.

Jessie didn't see me as I came around the corner. Mabel lay crumpled on the floor, her orange yarn hair stark against the white tile in the bathroom. Jessie'd hauled a chair over and was standing on it, staring in the mirror above the sink, her face all twisted and red, and she was saying to the mirror, over and over, "Damnation, damnation, damnation." Her fists were clenched and her feet planted wide on the chair.

"Jessie!" I said, snapping my fingers in front of her face. She didn't even flinch. Her eyes were blank and she was trembling. It scared me. I turned off the water and helped her down. Picked up Mabel and smoothed her hair. Handed her to Jessie, who clutched the doll to her chest, closed her eyes, and swayed as though music played. What did she hear that I couldn't hear? What did she see? Something was wrong. Terribly wrong.

Grandma and my mother were standing in the doorway, watching us.

"Can't you do something about her, Elvira? Make her stop saying that," my mother said, wringing her hands.

"It's not like I taught her the word. How am I supposed to stop her?" Lately, my mother had lost interest in Jessie, as though she didn't want to be the one blamed for making her strange. But I hadn't asked for a sister and I took the opportunity to point that out. "She's *your* daughter," I said. "You're the one who wanted her to talk."

"Fine, blame it on me," said my mother, walking away. "She'll probably turn out just like you, whining every hour of every day."

"Well, Jessie fits right in," Grandma said in a disgusted voice. "Nobody except me has any sense in this house."

I led Jessie to the supper table, settled her on her chair, and tucked a napkin under her chin. Buttered her biscuit and served her extra peas with pearl onions, her favorite. I suddenly felt sorry for her, being so different from regular kids. Maybe if I were nicer, she'd act more normal. I smoothed her curls and stroked her cheek with one finger. She shuddered for a second, then looked up at me and smiled a little smile like she wasn't just in the bathroom acting strange. Then she picked up a pearl onion between her thumb and forefinger, licked it, and popped it in her mouth.

Grandma clicked off *Amos 'n' Andy.* I knew I shouldn't expect it, but I'd hoped for a compliment on my biscuits since I'd added a dab of honey to the batter and they were particularly light and flaky. But Jessie's antics took center stage, as usual, and we ate supper all wrapped up in private thoughts, heads down while we chewed, the only sound the drip, drip, drip of the tap over the kitchen sink.

Jessie's second word was *surgery.* It came a few days later and she said it with the same enthusiasm, waving her hands around in circles as she marched. It was a Saturday; I'd finished my chores and was looking forward to an afternoon of quiet. My plan was to set up Jessie with our tin of Tiddledy-Winks. She liked to stack the chips in piles by color, knock them down, and start over. Usually kept her occupied for hours. Then I could escape to my closet and read, for lack of anything better, *The Bobbsey Twins in*

the Land of Cotton. I'd read it three times now, but it was all I had so I put up with the stomach-turning perfection of Bert, Nan, Freddie, and Flossie. There wasn't much room in the closet but I didn't mind being squished. I'd fixed up a corner by rolling our old Hudson Bay blanket and propping a pillow, and there was half a box of stale Saltines. At least I could hide from Jessie.

No such luck.

Sunlight streamed in through the living room window, and Jessie stopped in the middle of a patch, her eyes glassy, holding Mabel by the neck and shaking her. I thought Mabel's head might fly off, she was squeezing so hard. Jessie looked Mabel right in her blue-button eyes and shouted "surgery" as though she'd renamed her. By then, I was fourteen and had never even thought of using the word *surgery*. It wasn't a word that came up in everyday conversation like the words *chicken* or *bath*.

"That child is not normal," said Grandma to my mother as they both rushed in to see what all the fuss was about. "You were too old when you had her, addled her brain."

My mother had become quite good at ignoring Grandma and she did so, but she was worried, I could tell. I grabbed Jessie's hand, followed my mother to the kitchen, and gave Jessie a slice of bread to shut her up. Jessie broke off bits and pretended to feed Mabel, the glassy-eyed look gone and her lips sealed, for now. My mother plopped in her chair at the table, where she'd been shelling early peas, and her shoulders slumped and her feet turned in.

From there things went downhill fast.

Not that we'd ever gone uphill to prosperity, but we'd finally saved a little money, and we'd made it through spring eating Lutheran Ladies' Family Stew and corn bread. My mother was saving for a car. As she worked on the peas, she repeated her now-familiar speech on how if we had a car, she could get work in town. With the war over, men were back and they'd taken all the good jobs, but they wouldn't wash dishes in a diner and she would, come hell or high water. She was tired of being dirt-poor. And now that I was fourteen, I could get a job afternoons to help out. That was my mother's idea. I couldn't think of one thing I was good at, except reading, and who would pay a fourteen-year-old girl to read? My mother could wash all the dishes she wanted, but the thought of scraping food touched by some stranger's spitty mouth made me sick and I wouldn't do it.

I made the mistake of saying that out loud.

"Elvira," my mother said slowly, so the mad could build. "When I was your age, I did twice the chores you do and I didn't walk around all the time thinking I was better than everybody else." She wiped her hands on her apron as if talking made them sweaty. Or maybe to stop herself from wringing my neck.

Grandma, standing at the sink washing dishes, snorted.

"Yes, you did, Connie," she said. "That's exactly what you thought. You were so high and mighty, always worried about how you looked in the fancy dresses I slaved over, complaining the darts were off or the hemline was last year's fashion. Fussing over your hairdo like a *Collier's* photographer was knocking at the door. You cared most about which boy would follow you around that day. Chores were the last thing on your mind. Uppity's what you were."

Grandma turned from the sink, scrubbing one of our

chipped plates so hard her knuckles were white. "I used to smack you on the back to get your nose out of the air," she said. "You see yourself in Elvira. That's why you're picking on her all the time."

My mother frowned and shifted in her chair as though she could feel that smack on the back at that very moment. I knew she used to be beautiful and you could still see it in her face, melted chocolate eyes and wide mouth. Time and worry had done their work, though, and it was hard to imagine her young, followed by a pack of boys.

Grandma never left well enough alone.

"And then you had to go and fall for that fool Ray," she continued. "The worst of the lot. Backwoods family. All he ever did was sit around on that run-down porch, drinking whiskey and banging on his guitar. I tried to tell you but you were deaf to reason."

My stomach dropped and I felt queasy when my mother put her head down on the table, knocking the bowl of peas to the floor with her elbow. Even though I felt bad I'd started the fuss, I couldn't stop thinking how I'd have to pick up all those peas and wash them.

My mother started to cry. It occurred to me that maybe she missed my father, and I felt a catch in my throat. I still missed him too. But he'd been gone over four years and I'd pushed my memories aside.

Through all this Jessie'd been sitting quietly on the floor with Mabel in her lap, taking everything in like she always did. Listening. Watching. Sometimes she was so quiet we forgot she existed, but no sooner did my mother start to cry than Jessie unfolded her legs and strode over to stroke my mother's hand.

Jessie began to hum. A sweet little tune, mournful with low back-of-the-throat notes reaching up and dipping down, smooth and clear.

My mother raised her head and stared. She grabbed Jessie's shoulders and shook her. "Where'd you hear that song?" she whispered, her voice trembling.

"Ray," answered Jessie, as she went on humming.

"Ray" was Jessie's third word.

Chapter 4

Things might have been fine if we hadn't had a visit the very next day from the junk man. What you don't know can't hurt you.

He pulled up, truck full of clinking pans, tonics, buttons, and old books off someone's dusty shelves, looking to trade or buy or make a penny or two. He was big and black, and his white teeth gleamed behind thick lips when he smiled and rapped on the back door.

Grandma spoke to him through the screen. I smelled lilacs on the breeze.

"We don't need anything this month and there's nothing left to sell," she said.

The junk man looked at her sideways, his head cocked to his shoulder as if his neck was broken. The whites of his eyes were bloodshot. "Gossip for a quarter?" he asked. "Got good stories today."

For folks living way out in the middle of nowhere, local news was scarce. No one pinching pennies like we had to wasted money on a telephone, let alone newspapers, so when the junk man came, sometimes people would pay to catch up on what had been going on.

But I'd never seen Grandma pay a quarter for anything that wasn't absolutely necessary, so I was amazed when she said, "Elvira, fetch my pocketbook."

We trooped out and sat on the back steps to hear the junk man's gossip. I settled on the broken step so my mother wouldn't sit there. Might remind her of all the times she'd asked my father to fix it, and I didn't want to take a chance on spoiling the day. Jessie sat cross-legged on the ground, holding Mabel on her lap. She scooped a handful of dirt and trickled it over Mabel's legs. For once, Grandma didn't criticize. Mabel was already so dirty from Jessie's games there was no point.

I hoped we'd hear something that might give me an excuse to go to town alone. Maybe a socks and underwear sale too good to pass up at Mercer's Five and Dime. My mother might say yes to that. Then I could skip over to the library and see Mrs. Keller. Check out a new book. It would feel like a holiday. For a minute we could forget Jessie and her strange ways. A break from all the fretting was exactly what we needed. I turned my attention to the junk man, pulling my sweater close to ward off a shiver.

The junk man put his hands in the pockets of his overalls and rocked back and forth on his heels. He smelled. It drifted, came and went. Not a bad smell, exactly, but like old kitchen grease mixed with new grass. He stood off a ways, since we were female and white and it wouldn't be proper for him to sit down.

The first thing he told us was the Burns, our closest neigh-bors who lived up the highway two miles, had moved to Green Bay to live with their daughter since their only son had been killed in the war and they were too old and tired to run the farm anymore. They'd left the house more or less how it was and taken only a few trunks of clothes and pictures from when their life was easy. Mice had already moved in.

He told us about two new babies, one rich and one born at home to a poor family, like us. He said the poor one was prettier, blonde as sunlight with pink cheeks on pale skin, but the rich one had a fancy pram and its mother paraded up and down the sidewalk on DeWitt Street so all the folks eating lunch at Daisy's could admire her trim figure, aston-ishing after just giving birth.

Josie Crenshaw was the new operator for the Central State Telephone Company and was doing a fine job.

The sheriff had caught a teenaged boy stealing tires off the Cooper's spanking-new 1947 Pontiac. With the war over, tires weren't scarce so it truly didn't figure, Mr. Cooper said. Mrs. Cooper had always maintained that car shouldn't be parked on the street, so it just goes to show.

Someone broke a window at Rasmussen's Feed Store but nobody had been blamed. And the traveling preacher fell off the back of his truck when he forgot to set the hand brake, and the truck rolled down a ditch and smashed into a tree. He busted his head so bad one of his eyes popped right out of the socket and they had to do surgery over at the hospital to stick it back in. The preacher was recuperat-ing at this moment.

Grandma's head snapped up. "What kind of preacher?" she asked, even though the junk man had just finished tell-ing it.

The question threw him off his rhythm. "A traveling preacher, uh, the kind with no actual affiliation, I reckon," he said. "Been holding meetings down by the river so's to baptize believers right then and there. Working his way up to St. Paul's what I heard. Not going anywhere soon now, though. They say that preacher's surgery was tricky."

And right then, Jessie stood up and said, "Damnation."

My mother gasped and put her hand over her mouth, and I thought maybe she should put her hand on Jessie's mouth instead.

But Jessie went right on saying it and clenched her fists and stomped the ground. Her eyes glazed over. She snapped her head back and screamed to the sky, "If this is my punishment, then so be it, but lo, the sights to behold and the souls to save are walking the earth unguided, and I'll show them the light if you only let me see with both my eyes."

That was her first sentence.

The junk man's eyes got big and his jaw dropped, his mouth wide open like a dark cave. He backed away. Pointed a shaky finger at Jessie and said, "That's what that preacher said when they hauled him off to the hospital. Those exact words came right out of his mouth. She's got the third eye. She's a seer."

He flicked our quarter back at us, jumped in his truck, and was gone. I wasn't exactly sure what a seer was, but it couldn't be good, and I didn't want one for a sister.

Chapter 5

Looking back there had been signs and hints about Jessie, but it took me a lot of thought to get at them. They were buried deep where you hide what you don't want to see.

Jessie had seemed normal. A little shy maybe, or slow, and there was her silence for all that time, which maybe we should have paid more attention to. But still, normal mostly, and I'd thought surely there were other kids like her. She was little and pretty, and on the day of the junk man she was only four and a half. Even though she was a shadow on my heels, four and a half years is not a lot of time to study a person's habits.

But normal kids don't hear songs strummed by their dead father, and they don't rant and rave and stomp like preachers. Even Grandma had to admit that Jessie couldn't possibly know all the words she used in that sentence. "What kind of child says, 'the sights to behold and the souls to save are walking the earth unguided,' for pity's sake," she said. But she couldn't explain it. Neither could my mother and she brushed away my questions with a wave of a hand and a sigh.

I crept into our room. Jessie slept, tucked under the old blue-and-yellow wedding-ring quilt on the bed we'd shared since she was a baby. She looked peaceful, her curls all spread out, still damp and smelling clean from the bath I'd given her after supper. She cradled Mabel and the orange hair splayed on the pale skin of her arm. I clicked off the closet light and crawled in beside her.

Jessie slept hard. She never seemed to dream.

I, on the other hand, dreamed a lot, especially one dream that kept coming back. A dream of drowning on a gloomy, gray day and my father standing above, waving, not even trying to save me as I went under, blubbering and spewing water through my nose. I called out to him as I sank into darkness.

And then, under the water, an orange flash like the sun fell in and stayed stuck there, unable to return to warm the sky. I always woke from that dream covered in sweat, wet like I'd actually been in water, heart pounding, glad to find myself in my own bed, my sister curled in a ball and breathing softly in and out, the windowsill shining from silver moonlight slipping through the lace curtains.

But Jessie didn't dream. Not at night. Instead, she left our presence during the day when she was wide-awake, sometimes sitting right beside me. No warning. I'd be doing algebra homework, my book open beside me on the sofa, my notebook on my lap, and Jessie's eyes would glaze over and she'd go rigid. As if she were under a spell. Where did she go when she was dazed like that? I'd snap my fingers in front of her face or clap, loudly, to get her attention, but she never flinched or woke up until she was ready or done with whatever it was she'd seen. Then she'd stare at me as though I were crazy.

That troubled me. "What?" I always asked. "Why are you looking at me like that? I'm not crazy." Every time, I'd wondered if Jessie's trance was my imagination. But now I knew it wasn't.

Jessie was fascinated by light. Light from lamps drew her like it draws bugs. She liked unexpected light: the round dial on the radio or tiny bits of light like the narrow slit of yellow under a closed door. She liked to watch bright patches skipping on the ground as leaves shifting on a breeze made space for sunshine to pass through. Flames mesmerized her. I often found her staring until the wood in the fireplace burned down to a chalky gray, the leftover red glow reflecting in her eyes.

Jessie loved to spin. She'd find a sunbeam streaming through a window, dust particles swirling like trash in a devil dance, and she'd jump smack in the middle and twirl. Eyes closed, arms straight out, she'd twirl until she was so dizzy she'd flop to the floor. Then she'd shake her head to get the dizzy out.

And there was the time Jessie took the knife. It was my mother's big meat knife with a razor-sharp blade, the one she never even let me use. It had a thick, black bone handle held together with screws that were constantly loosening, my mother grumbling each time she fetched a screwdriver to tighten them.

But one day it was gone. Jessie and I were sitting at the

kitchen table shucking corn, dropping the husks and silks into the compost can. My mother had a frying chicken on the cutting board and was rummaging through drawers. "Where in the Sam Hill is my meat knife?" she asked, and I saw Jessie dip her head as though she'd been caught stealing an extra cookie. "Elvira, did you put it somewhere? You know you're not supposed to use it."

It figured she'd blame me. "I didn't touch it," I said, poking Jessie and wondering why she wouldn't look at me. My mother, impatient to get on with supper, pulled out the saw knife, complaining as she carved that it wasn't as sharp and would never cut through the gristle. And then the saw knife slipped. My mother gave a little cry. It wasn't a very deep cut and a quick rinse stopped the bleeding. Grandma wrapped a Band-Aid around my mother's finger and my mother continued cutting the chicken, griping the whole while about how dull that knife was.

I lifted Jessie's chin so she'd have to look me in the eye. If my mother had been using the razor-sharp meat knife she would have lost a finger. I knew it. Jessie knew it, I could tell. Behind my mother's and Grandma's back I mouthed, *Where is it?* Jessie reached into the compost can, parting the corn husks, and at the bottom of the can was the knife. She smiled.

So I knew the junk man was right.

Jessie was a seer.

It occurred to me it was a good thing we lived out in the middle of nowhere, because that junk man would spread the gossip of Jessie's seeing powers all over Columbia County by morning and most people would never find our house if they were inclined to look.

❦

Even from our room I could hear the anxious tone in my mother's voice. I slid out from under the quilt, careful not to disturb Jessie. I felt I had a right to participate in the discussion my mother and Grandma were having at the kitchen table that night.

Grandma disagreed.

"Elvira," she said, "you go back to bed. You're too young to understand any of this."

That made me mad and I said, "I'm the one taking care of her all the time. I never even have a moment to myself."

Sometimes comments backfire. That one did and Grandma jumped at it.

"Why don't you take *this* moment to yourself then and get on out of here, like I told you," she said. "And quit your sassing." She rolled up a dish towel and swatted the air toward my bottom.

It was always clear Grandma liked to be in charge. My mother sat like a bump on a log, not even looking up, picking at a chip in the table with her fingernail. I felt sorry for her. Maybe I'd try to be nicer since she had so many problems right then and her own mother wasn't offering much comfort.

I pretended to leave in a huff with a stomp to my step for good measure, but I stopped down the hall to eavesdrop. I couldn't believe what I heard.

"Connie, we have to send her away," said Grandma. "It's for her own good. And ours. If we don't, we'll be shunned in town worse than you already are thanks to that drinking fool of a husband and his fits of fury. Besides, you could never let her go to school. The kids would beat the living daylights out of her. You know I'm right. Don't make another mistake like the one you made having her in the first place, and marrying her father before that."

I heard Grandma pacing, slippers flapping. She had to point out my mother's mistakes again. My stomach flipped when I realized even I was starting to think of my mother having Jessie and marrying my father as mistakes.

But my mother stood up for herself that time. Her voice was strong. Defiant.

"No," she said. "I'm not sending Jessie away. We'll all go."

Chapter 6

My mother leaped into action, moving at a pace one step down from frantic. I'd never seen her like that. She kept the radio on full volume. Frank Sinatra crooning through the static spurred her on. With only three days left until summer vacation, I stayed home from school and helped her make lists. Nothing but parties the last days of school anyway. For parties you needed someone to sit next to and a mother who made cupcakes.

I kept asking why we had to leave and where we were going, but my mother ignored those questions. I wouldn't miss Portage. But I'd miss Mrs. Keller and the library. And how could I leave this house? Or my father? I wandered through the rooms as though the ghost of him might appear. Ran my finger along the dusty windowsill in the living room. Stared through the glass at the front yard. So many times I'd imagined my father's boots pounding the steps, the bang of the screen door, and the whistle that meant his spirits were up. Those sounds were like a favorite tune stuck in my mind. If I left this house, would I ever hear them again? Grandma said, "A house is just a house, and they're a dime a dozen." But to me, this house was home when my father was in it.

I found one of his old black socks in the dust under the sofa. There was a hole in the heel, and I stuck my finger through it, wondering what had happened to the other sock. My mother was clearing out kitchen cupboards, hauling boxes up and down the basement stairs every five seconds, blind to my presence, and Jessie was helping Grandma untangle thread and rickrack. I tiptoed to my closet, my father's sock stuffed in the back pocket of my overalls. I darned the hole with my best stitches and put my treasures into it.

My treasures were little things we'd discovered on walks in the woods. A tiny pinecone. A dove-gray agate with white swirls and black dots that looked like moss. A scrub jay feather and a brass button. I stuffed his sock with the treasures into my underwear drawer. No one would look there since it was my chore to pull the wash down from the line in the basement, fold it, and put it all away, and soon it wouldn't matter where I hid my treasures, because we were leaving this place. It already felt empty. My mother was in and out the next few days, hitching into town to pick up food and supplies. She was gone for hours, walking or begging rides back. The reception she got in Portage was cold and she said people wouldn't look at her. Kept whispering behind her back.

"What little money I have is as good as theirs," she said.

"Who are they to question? Those old biddies hang on to gossip like it's the only thing keeping them alive." It bothered her, though. She stuffed towels into a box without refolding and kicked the box to a corner.

People had always talked about us behind our backs. That wasn't new.

Days when I used to go to town with my father, they'd point a finger and cross the street before they even smelled the whiskey on his breath. As if he'd pick a fight with anyone, me standing right there. I knew my father had a temper. I knew his drinking made it worse. He'd bloodied noses and punched stomachs and landed behind bars more than once for public drunkenness and disorderly conduct. I'd heard my mother crying in the middle of the night the times she'd had to take money from the savings jar and walk to town to bail him out.

I knew those were the stories the townsfolk told. It was why I didn't have any friends. None of the mothers would let their children be friends with someone whose father might beat up their dad someday.

I almost had a friend once. She started out nice enough. It was the first day of school, second grade. Summer heat was holding on and the window near my seat in the old school bus was stuck, dirt or damage keeping it from sliding down. I struggled and banged but it wouldn't budge.

"Want some help with that?"

I'd seen her the previous year on the playground but she wasn't in my class. Her name was Julia, and once I got a taste of her, I always wondered how such a pretty name could go with a mean streak like she had.

"Sure," I said. "Thanks."

45

"You take one side, I'll take the other, and we'll both pull down hard at the same time. Ready?"

The window gave and a rush of air swept stray hairs back, tickling my ears. The bus jerked forward and Julia plopped down next to me. I'd never had a seatmate before.

"What's your name?" she asked.

"Elvira Witsil," I said.

Julia got a sickly look on her face, as if she had a bad stomach or she'd eaten rotten eggs for breakfast and just recalled the smell.

"Your dad's the lush, right?"

I'd never heard that word. But from the way she said it, I knew it was something bad.

"My father's not a lush," I said. "*Your* father's a lush."

"Is not," she said. "My daddy never touches a drop of drink. My mother said for me to stay away from you. She said your father is crazy and crazy in a family is catching, like cooties. You'd better not touch me."

I punched her hard in the arm.

And of course she hollered so loud Mr. Wilson slammed on the brakes and the bus screeched to a stop, all our book bags sliding and kids slipping off balance because they'd all turned to look at Julia and me fighting in the back.

Mr. Wilson had been the bus driver forever, and it was his personal mission to convert us all to religion. "God bless you," he'd say to every one of us as we stepped off the bus each day. "Say your prayers and thank your mother for giving you life."

So he made Julia and me stand in the aisle in front of everyone and shake hands or walk the rest of the way. Our choice.

We shook. Julia squeezed my hand until it hurt.

"You two must forgive each other," said Mr. Wilson, "whatever your differences."

I'd never forgive Julia. I hated her. I hated her perfect father and her nosy mother. I hated her for what she said about my father.

It wasn't like I didn't know before. I'd smelled the whiskey. Knew he disappeared. I thought it was my fault. Each time he came back I was extra nice. Brought him coffee and cleared the supper dishes, taking care not to be loud. Hoping I'd be his reason to stay. Hoping he'd stop needing whiskey so my mother wouldn't yell anymore. Sometimes I tiptoed, afraid the click of my shoes would set her off. Each time he came back, my mother would lock the door to their bedroom, and it didn't open until he told enough jokes and she was drawn by his laugh. Then I knew everything was okay.

But mostly, that day, the day I was told my father was a lush, I hated my mother for giving me life, and from then on, I stopped wanting friends too.

And the talk didn't stop with Julia. I heard it the next year, and the next, on the playground at school, in the market while shopping with my mother, and even once in line at the bank. People would turn away when I stared them down, but I'd heard the words and they knew it. I was used to my father and his drinking being the talk of the town and mostly I closed my ears to it.

But having a seer in the family was worse. That would scare everyone in Portage. They'd worry Jessie would know their thoughts or hear their prayers. Tell their secrets.

47

My mother arranged to sell off the rest of our furniture to our landlord in exchange for back rent, keeping only bedding, the last of her china dishes, the cast-iron skillets, the coffeepot, and clothes we couldn't live without. In less than a week she was ready to go. She tried to throw away my father's old brown parka, saying we wouldn't need it where we were going. But I dug it from the garbage and hid it at the bottom of my box. I got my sock full of treasures from my underwear drawer and tucked the sock in the pocket of the parka.

My mother insisted I take a schoolbook with me. I flipped through my *Gregg Shorthand* book. She had it in her head I'd be a secretary someday, typing sixty words per minute and a master at shorthand thanks to the wonderful instruction in *Gregg Shorthand*. "If you're going to have your nose in a book, it may as well be something useful," she always said. "I never had opportunities. Consider yourself lucky."

I didn't feel lucky. Typing was dull and I hated shorthand; all the squiggly lines reminded me of worms. I tossed the shorthand book in the garbage, jumping as Jessie came up behind me and tugged on my overalls. She handed me the *Lutheran Ladies' Guild Cookbook*. Jessie was right. I still loved to flip through the dessert section. Looking at the checkered cover, I remembered the white-haired church lady, how she'd smiled and handed it to me. That cookbook really was mine. I put it in my box.

I couldn't sort out my feelings. Nothing was holding me in Portage. I should have been happy to go. But my stomach was heavy with a nagging sense of forgetting something. I checked and rechecked my list but I'd packed everything my mother told me to take except the short-hand book. That wasn't it.

I heard my father's voice in my head. "Race," he'd always say, taking off down the path behind the house. I'd chase after him but he never let me win. He made it to our secret spot before me every time. "Slowpoke," he'd laugh, leaning on our rock, arms folded as though he'd been waiting forever.

I had to see that place one more time. I ran out back, past the garden, and down the path. Sun had warmed the surface of our rock. When I climbed up and lay back flat, hands under my head like my father and I had always done, I felt the warmth through my entire body. I'd hardly been there in the years since Jessie was born. The rock was exactly as I remembered — a smooth, old granite boulder in a little clearing surrounded by birch and maple and Norway pines.

This was our special place. We'd spent hours lying on the rock, away from my mother and chores, watching the zigzag course of a dragonfly, listening to the whirring of the wind and the birds chirping and each other's breathing.

Sometimes we sang songs.

My father would whistle a tune and then he'd say, "C'mon, Elvira, what's the title of that song? Think hard now."

His favorite was "Blueberry Hill" by Glenn Miller. He always started off with that one so I'd get my first guess right. "Blueberry Hill" was my favorite song too. Something catchy about that tune. I'd find myself drumming my fingers or tapping my foot to the beat long after my father had whistled it. He taught me the words to other songs he knew from the radio, songs about love and war and places we wished we could see, but "Blueberry Hill" stayed with me.

Except for Grandma's criticizing, nobody ever talked about my father. It seemed I was the only one who remembered anything good about him. Leaving that rock was leaving my father behind forever.

Maybe he wasn't dead. What if at this very moment he was traveling on foot from some place far away, tired and hungry and lonely, trying to get back home? How would he find us if we left?

I slipped off the rock and picked up a sharp stone. If my father came back to Portage, he'd come here. I scratched my name into the surface of the boulder. Then I scratched the words *I'm sorry* above my name. It was the best I could do. Someday I'd come back. Maybe he'd be here, whistling "Blueberry Hill." Waiting for me.

My mother called and even with the distance, her tone made it clear she was annoyed at my absence.

I pressed my cheek to the smooth surface of our rock one last time, then dragged my feet toward the house, feeling empty and tired, "Blueberry Hill" repeating over and over in my head. Even that song couldn't drown out the voice reminding me of the guilt I carried. Nothing could.

My mother called again. What would she do if I ignored her? What *could* she do — leave me behind? I left the path, skirting the edge of the woods, and headed toward the highway to town, breaking into a run that kicked up dust and dry leaves. It was still early. I could be back in a few hours. There was one person I needed to see before I'd let my mother drag me off to nowhere.

༆

The Portage Library on MacFarlane Road was a grand Victorian donated to the town by some rich man in the olden days. The wide steps led to double doors that squeaked on brass hinges as I pulled the handle. The familiar smell of leather-bound books and floor polish and the mustiness of old wooden shelves made my heart leap with happiness. Sunlight shone through high paned windows, making slanted squares on the red Oriental rug in front of the reading chairs. A man turned the pages of a newspaper, his round glasses reflecting the light. He didn't look up as I passed.

Mrs. Keller wasn't at her desk. For a second I panicked, but then I saw her at the card file, pulling yellowed rectangles out of the drawer slots and making notes on them with the pen that hung on a chain around her neck.

"Hi, Mrs. Keller," I said. I'd forgotten to comb my mousy-brown hair and rebraid it this morning, and suddenly I was self-conscious of too many freckles that Grandma always said made me look partially cooked. Mrs. Keller always looked crisp and neat; her short blonde hair was shiny and crimped in waves, and her sweater sets perfectly matched one line of the plaid in her pleated skirts. She always wore sensible pumps and rayon stockings even though most ladies had gone back to nylon or silk. Today's sweater set was a pale green like spring grass. It was a color my mother never wore.

"Elvira! I am so glad to see you," she said in a library whisper but clapping her hands like a little kid. "I was beginning to wonder if you had flown the coop." Her laugh was like bells. It had been ages since I'd missed the school bus on purpose to spend an hour at the library, but she'd noticed my absence. It made what I came to say even harder, and sadness settled in the pit of my stomach.

I wanted to tell her all of it: my father and his drinking, the mean ways of my mother and Grandma, how my father was gone because of me. I wanted to tell her about my strange sister and explain what the junk man said. Mrs. Keller didn't know any of that. That was why she liked me. She didn't know the real me.

"We're leaving," I said instead. "I wanted to say good-bye."

Mrs. Keller shut the card file drawer, took my elbow, and led me over to her desk, pointing to the straight-back oak chair where I'd spent hours copying new titles and authors' names onto cards using my best cursive. Mrs. Keller said my penmanship was impeccable.

I sat, jiggling my leg and not looking at her. Mrs. Keller rolled her chair close to mine so we could whisper. "Where are you going?"

"I don't know." It sounded so stupid.

Mrs. Keller smoothed her skirt and straightened a pile of books on her desk. She reached out and lifted my chin to look me in the eyes. "Nobody should have to move away without a good-bye gift from a friend, don't you think?"

Tears stung and I looked at the floor. I heard her pumps clicking but she was only gone a minute. She came back carrying a thick volume, sat back down, and opened a drawer in her desk, the wood scraping like fingernails on a blackboard. "Darn that drawer," she whispered, looking around to see if anyone had been disturbed by the sound. She pulled out a Baby Ruth bar and, keeping her hands below the desk so no one could see, unwrapped it to break off a hunk. I was amazed. No food in the library was her biggest rule, next to no talking.

I thought she was going to give me the hunk of Baby Ruth, but instead she opened the book on her desk and smeared the chocolate across the title page. "Oh dear," she said, rubbing in the brown streak with her fingertips. "This book is damaged. How sad. I'll have to mark it as a discard. Here's the card file, Elvira. Will you please stamp it?"

She handed me the discard stamp and that was when I saw the title. *A Tree Grows in Brooklyn* by Betty Smith.

"The main character reminds me of you, Elvira," she said. "She has her troubles but she's not afraid of an adventure and she ends up stronger for it. May God watch over you on your journey." Mrs. Keller stood up. Patted my shoulder.

I hugged the book to my chest as I stood up too. "I'll read it a hundred times."

"That's the spirit," said Mrs. Keller.

Chapter 7

"Where've you been?"

My mother stood at the bottom of the back steps, hands on her hips. Her cheeks were pink as if she'd gussied up with too much rouge, but I knew the flush meant she was angry or nervous. I usually avoided her when she had pink cheeks. I noticed she'd changed into her favorite yellow-and-gray plaid shirtwaist with a wide belt that made her look thin, pinned her hair in a French twist, and applied red lipstick. She hadn't worn lipstick for a long time. That was odd.

"Thinking," I said, trying to dodge my mother's glare by kneeling down to tie my sneaker. *A Tree Grows in Brooklyn* was stuffed in the front of my overalls right next to the pain in my heart. "I lost track of time."

"There's no time for daydreaming, Elvira. It's almost

one o'clock. Make yourself useful and carry some boxes out to the front porch. I'm tired of your lazy behavior."

"It's not fair we have to leave because of Jessie," I said, instead of reminding my mother she gave me so many chores I never had time to be lazy. She just never noticed me unless I was working or in trouble. And who cared if it was one o'clock? Nobody mentioned there was any big rush. "Maybe she's not a seer. Maybe that junk man was wrong. Why can't we stay?"

"Stop asking the same thing over and over," she said with a dramatic sigh. "You're giving me a headache. Whining never gets you anywhere in this world. Go find Jessie. Both of you get cleaned up. And put on a dress for once."

She turned and stomped up the steps. A dress? Why would I put on a dress? All we were doing was packing up and getting dirty. There was nothing wrong with overalls. I could tell by her no-nonsense tone that I'd better do it, though. It amazed me how much my mother sounded and acted like Grandma sometimes.

Grandma had been fuming and muttering under her breath for days, but she helped pack and she wasn't refusing to leave. Jessie was all caught up in the excitement and ran around in circles waving her arms.

I snagged her mid-twirl. "Come on, Jessie. Let's see if we can find a pretty dress for you." I tried to keep the disgust I felt about dresses out of my voice. Maybe Jessie would grow up to like them and be one of those prissy ladies whose hats and shoes and gloves always matched whatever they wore. I doubted it, though, looking at the tangles in her curls and the smudges of dirt on her cheeks. If anything, Mabel was a good indication of Jessie's future fashion sense. Poor Mabel was filthy.

I put Jessie in a pink organdy party dress that Grandma said she'd made for me when I was Jessie's age. As far as I remembered, there'd been no occasion for me to wear it, so the dress was in pretty good shape, and it fit Jessie perfectly. It had puffy sleeves and a white Peter Pan collar with a satin belt that made a big bow when tied in the back. It was much too fancy for packing up. What was my mother up to? Jessie didn't fuss, though. She stood still as I tied the bow and giggled but didn't squirm when I pulled lace-topped socks over her ticklish toes. She insisted on fastening the buckles on her patent leather Mary Janes herself, struggling to get the tab through the tiny hole in the strap. I was running out of patience, but she pushed my hand away when I tried to do it for her.

"Hurry up then," I said. "We still have to wash those dirty hands."

Jessie didn't like the feel of water on her hands or face. She scowled while I scrubbed. Her expression made me laugh. "You look like a grouchy, old bear," I said, dipping the washcloth in warm water and rubbing between her fingers where dirt was caked. The sink looked like a mud puddle after the third dip. I probably should have dressed her after the wash but it was too late now.

Jessie hadn't said any words since the junk man's visit. I wished she'd talk to me. It would be nice to have someone to talk to.

"Where do *you* think we're going, Jessie?" I asked as I tugged the brush through her tangles.

Her green eyes got wide. She knew.

"Tell me," I said, and my heart started to pound. Why was I scared? I was rougher with the brush than I intended and Jessie flinched. "Tell me where we're going. Please."

Jessie stared. Silent. Clutched Mabel to her bony little chest and wrenched her eyes away as though it was painful to look at me. "What?" I said. "What is it?" Jessie shook her head and ran from the bathroom, her Mary Janes clicking on the hardwood floor.

I didn't follow. I slid to the floor, closed my eyes, and wished with all my might I knew how to pray for answers to all my questions. Mrs. Keller believed in God. She'd said, "May God watch over you on your journey," and somehow, I knew she meant it. But nobody believed in God in my house. The only other person I knew who believed in God was old Mr. Wilson, the school bus driver. "God bless you," he still said every day. "Say your prayers." But he never told us *how* to pray.

Was God real? He couldn't be. What kind of God would take someone's father? But that wouldn't be God's fault. It was mine. What kind of God would let a mother keep secrets? It wasn't fair that I was the only one wishing we could stay in Portage and at the same time wondering where we were going and how we were getting there.

But since no one would tell me no matter how much I badgered, I picked myself up, washed my face and hands, scrubbed until I thought skin might peel and freckles would fade. Yanked my least-favorite school dress over my head. Left my sneakers on and didn't change my socks. Didn't comb out my braid, either, but my mother said nothing. She seemed distracted. Jumpy. Kept fussing with her hair and smoothing her dress. As though she had someone to impress.

Grandma wasn't wearing a dress. She wore men's trousers and a light-blue blouse with the sleeves rolled up. Not much could get Grandma in a dress. Maybe a funeral. I guess we were alike in that one way.

For an hour or two, Jessie clung to my mother's side, avoiding my glare, while Grandma and I hefted boxes and stacked them on the porch.

It wasn't until an ancient red truck on skinny tires with a dent in the bumper pulled up to the front door, right over the dead lawn, that I finally got an inkling of what was going on.

I knew who it was the minute he stepped onto the porch. Before he raised his hand to knock. Before Jessie said "damnation."

The traveling preacher wore a black patch over the eye that had been sewn back in and his once-white suit was dusty and threadbare; his shoes were boots with a pointy toe, not at all the kind of shoes most men would wear with a suit. He carried a black fedora with a gray-and-white – striped band around the middle and a crease in the crown. His brown hair was matted from wearing it. He looked like a gangster down on his luck.

But his smile was wide when he saw me sneaking a peek through the front window. Why was he smiling at me?

He gave a little wave and pointed to the door. Raised his eyebrows.

I couldn't move.

But Jessie could. She ran to the door and flung it open.

"Damnation," she said, like that was his name. Jessie bounced excitedly, the bow of her dress coming untied. Mabel dangled upside down from Jessie's fingers as though the doll were trying to escape. Then Jessie pointed to the preacher's eye patch. "Is that where your eye got poked out?" she asked.

He laughed. Touched his eye patch like he'd just remembered it was there. My mother came out to the porch and handed the preacher a cup of coffee. As though she'd been expecting him. Did he like it black or with milk and sugar, and how did she know? Even Grandma greeted him with a nod. I slunk back against the living room wall.

The preacher patted Jessie on the head and she took his hand. The two of them stepped over the threshold into our empty house.

From then on Jessie talked a regular blue streak.

Chapter 8

The preacher drove at a snail's pace on US 51, then rumbled off on old Highway 16, and by the second day we'd only hit the outskirts of Eau Claire. We'd passed the Dells, rivers and woods, bumped through towns even tinier than Portage with one main street and nothing else to see, and we'd skirted at least a dozen of Wisconsin's thousands of lakes. Every mosquito that lived in the state had tried to bite me. When we stopped for gasoline, the preacher peeled bits of wings and the guts of wasps and flies off the bug screen attached to the front of the truck.

Jessie and I rode in the back, shoulder to shoulder, knocking around with all our boxes, sucking in dust and exhaust. I tried to keep my nose covered with our Hudson Bay blanket, but it was making me hot and itchy. Every bump knocked me into Jessie. She didn't seem at all disturbed by the jostling or the dust or the fact that we were traveling with some man we didn't know, headed to who knows where and sleeping in a tent on the rocky ground at night. But Jessie *did* know where we were going. I was the one left in the dark. I wanted to shake it out of her. She sat there hugging Mabel, humming a tune I could barely hear over the rattle of the preacher's truck, as if she hadn't a care in the world.

It wasn't as warm up north as it had been at home even though it was June. The air smelled of new grass and felt humid like a storm was brewing, but the sky was big and blue with only a few fluffy white clouds. No thunder-heads. I turned my back on Jessie so she'd know I was annoyed with her, folded the blanket to make a cushion, and watched the countryside flash past in a blur of gold and green.

It was pretty here. Different than home. Apple orchards were budding out, trunks gnarled like old fingers and white blossoms scattered like swirls of snow as they dropped on dark, rich soil. If I were a baby bird, I'd want my mother and father to build a nest for me in an apple tree. I couldn't imagine a better place to learn to fly. Someday I'd have an apple tree. Maybe I'd have an entire orchard on a farm like the ones we passed, with sprawling fields, vegetable gardens, big red barns, and fruit trees as far as you could see. Then I could choose a different tree every day and climb it, lie in the crook of a branch in the leafy shade and read.

I hadn't even had a chance to open *A Tree Grows in Brooklyn*. It was buried in my box and, although I could get to it if I stretched, the words on the page would jiggle and jump and I'd probably get carsick. Besides, if my mother or Grandma turned around and looked through the cab window, I'd be caught with the book. One of them would take it away, no doubt. The book would have to wait.

Along the road, early wildflowers were waiting to make sure the nights were safe from frost before blooming, all curled up like they had their hands over their heads. I knew how they felt. I wanted to crawl in a hole in the ground and hide until it was safe to come out.

I'd been throwing questions at my mother and grandma at every opportunity, still hoping for an answer. Questions like where were we going and why, and would we have to help the preacher hold sermons because I didn't believe in God and wouldn't that be lying?

My mother wouldn't budge and Grandma answered, "Never mind."

I didn't ask Jessie again. Grandma was right about one thing. Jessie was stubborn. She wasn't going to tell me where we were going.

I didn't like it. I didn't like it one bit.

But Jessie did. She was a different person, smiling and chattering like never before. She took to that preacher right off, following him around and sitting down beside him when we stopped to camp the first night and my mother was busy starting supper. Jessie touched his arm, stroked it gently as if that would keep him from getting up and leaving. He didn't seem to mind, patted her on the head absentmindedly while he whittled a thick stick with his pocketknife, shavings piling up at his feet.

"You're a friendly little thing," he said.

"Friendly," Jessie echoed.

The preacher laughed. He had a deep voice, surprising because he wasn't very big. Out of all of us, he could use the most fattening up. Seeing Jessie sitting there with that preacher sent a wave of jealousy through my body. It stuck in my craw she was giving him all that attention. Even though I spent a lot of time trying to get rid of Jessie when she shadowed my heels, I didn't want her to like that preacher. He couldn't take care of her like I could.

"What are you making?" Jessie asked, sidling in for a closer look.

"A whistle," he said. "I'll show you how to play a snappy tune when it's finished. Would you like that?"

Jessie jumped up and hopped on one foot, something I'd recently taught her. "Oh yes. I'd love to play a snappy tune."

They all laughed. Even Grandma. I wondered if the preacher had secretly traded the family I knew for some other family that looked like mine.

The preacher never talked to me. He smiled and nodded but that was all. Of course, I wasn't real sociable and I didn't trust him the way my mother and Jessie seemed to. My mother talked to him like they were old friends. They stopped talking when I came near and didn't include me in their conversations. I was supposed to be seen and not heard. But she looked that preacher directly in the face and smiled and touched his arm lightly with her fingertips. Like she was flirting.

So by the second day we were only to Eau Claire, and I'd had time to think.

At dusk, the preacher pulled off the highway into a clump of willows, and everyone but me jumped out, stretching and shaking stiff legs to get the circulation going. Hundreds of fireflies flitted, dipping and rising like sparks from a campfire. Jessie raced off to catch one, cupping it in her hands gently like I'd taught her. Pink light washed over a clearing in the grove and a creek bubbled over rocks perfectly placed for stepping. It would be fun to explore. Catch skitters on the surface of the water. Trap a few crawdads. My father caught crawdads in the creek at the bottom of our rocky dell. They were fast and furious, but he caught them with his bare hands. Then he'd say, "A creature this feisty deserves the home it was given." And he'd put it back, satisfied as it scurried to hide.

Had my father believed in God?

The first star appeared, blinking under a sliver of pale moon. *Star light, star bright ... what is the point of wishing tonight?* I didn't move. Sat in the back of the truck, my bottom sore.

I wanted answers.

"Elvira," said Grandma in a threatening voice, as though she'd wallop me whether the preacher was watching or not. "You get on out here and gather some wood."

I ignored her.

My mother tried. "Come help, Elvira." Her voice was sweet, pleading, as if she always talked to me nicely and wasn't usually blind to my existence. "Aren't you hungry?"

I *was* hungry. We'd only had cheese and bread and that had been hours before. But I didn't move.

They left me alone and set up camp without my help. Grandma put up the two tents, both belonging to the preacher, heavy green canvas over metal poles with stakes to hold the corners down and zipper flaps for doors. Jessie scampered back and forth gathering sticks for kindling and hefting rocks as big as she was to make a circle for the fire. My mother started supper. The preacher walked down to the creek and filled our old enamel coffeepot and a pan for washing dishes, sloshing as he struggled back. I watched the bustling activity feeling strangely left out.

Soon, the smell of bacon frying made my stomach rumble. My mother brought me a plate of beans and bread and two thick slices of country bacon, still sizzling. I was astounded. At home, we'd always had to get our own plate. She tugged the tailgate and it banged down with a squeal. She perched on the edge, swinging her legs, her back to me. Light from the campfire flickered, the shadows of the willows long threads weaving on the ground. My mother turned to face me, her expression calm, happy. Why was she in such a good mood?

I chewed and waited for her to say something. She was quiet for so long I had plenty of time to prepare my own speech. "I'm not getting out of this truck until you tell me where we're going, and I'm not helping with anything until you explain why we're going wherever it is we're going," I said. After I spit it out, I thought I could have said it better. Used a few big words to show I was serious.

"Elvira," she answered, drawing one leg up and tucking it neatly under her dress. "I'll tell you, but I don't want any fussing or back talk. My mind's made up."

I was so surprised she'd agreed to tell me I didn't say anything for fear she'd change her tune.

"In the morning, we're going into St. Paul for a meeting, sort of a revival, and then we're driving west," she said, swatting at a mosquito. It buzzed over to me and landed. I let it suck until its sack filled and then smashed it on my arm. Licked my finger and wiped the blood. My mother frowned but continued. "We're going as far as the Pacific Ocean, Elvira. To California. Where it's warm."

My mother smoothed her cotton shirtwaist as if her hands would iron out the wrinkles from sitting all day. Wisps of hair escaped from her braid. She looked like a war amputee, one leg dangling and just the knee show-ing of the other. The thought of it made me a little sick, but I wondered what it would be like to hop around on one leg all the time because you had to, not just for fun. I wondered what one-legged soldiers did with the other shoe since shoes always came in pairs. Didn't seem fair, the waste of money. Did my father know any one-legged soldiers when he was on the ship? I'd take a one-legged father over a missing one any day.

My mind snapped back when my mother's voice got sharp.

"Elvira," she said, crossing her arms. "Are you listening?"

"I'm listening." But I knew I wasn't going to like what I was about to hear.

"The preacher wants us to work with him, helping people, um, understand themselves better. You know how long it's been since we had any money, Elvira. I'm plain tired of that. We'll be letting people come to Jessie and with her being a seer, she'll help them in all kinds of ways." She raised her eyebrows and spread her hands wide as though anyone who couldn't see the benefits might be stupid. "The preacher says Jessie has a gift. I think it would be wrong to waste it. Selfish. He says Jessie's gift is God's plan."

God's plan? I'd never heard my mother speak of God in that way. As if there was a map we should all follow. She didn't even believe in God. Why had she agreed to travel with a preacher? And then I figured it out. My mother's intention was to charge for Jessie's seeing capabilities. Make money off my sister's gift or insight or third eye or any old name you gave it. I could see the guilt in my mother's face, the knowing it was wrong. I also saw her mind was set.

That preacher had duped my mother good.

"Why?" I asked, biting off a hunk of bacon but finding it hard to swallow.

I wanted more. I wanted her to give me a reason to believe in her. I wanted to hear her say nobody would get hurt, she'd take care of us, and even though our life was odd, it would be normal in the end. I wanted her to take some blame for the way things were.

It would be so embarrassing traveling the country with people coming to my sister and her only four and knowing more than me, giving advice to grown-ups too stupid to think for themselves. Just where did I fit in to all that? But I didn't say those thoughts out loud.

Instead I said, "Why would you let that preacher put Jessie in front of a bunch of strangers like she's some circus-freak fortune-teller? We don't need money that bad. I'll get a job if you take us home." I wouldn't wash spitty dishes, though. I left that fact out. Let her think I would.

But she was not going to budge.

"I've got my reasons," answered my mother. "And my reasons are private. That's all I'm going to say." She got up, smoothed her dress again, and a shiver shook her body. She folded her arms to protect from a chill, either an imaginary one or a drop in temperature, I couldn't tell, and walked away.

And then I saw where I fit in. It was up to me to keep

Jessie safe. Like it or not, I was the one taking care of her. I was the one she'd always depended on. Not that preacher. He wasn't family. He couldn't be trusted and neither could my mother. So I vowed then and there, no matter what, I'd protect Jessie from harm.

But what I really wanted was someone to protect me.

Chapter 9

It took a long time for me to fall asleep that night, and when I finally did, it seemed like only minutes had passed and I was awake again. I'd had the dream. I sat up, damp from sweat, shivering in the freezing air, the tent walls casting strange green shadows with the first rays of dawn. My heart sank when I realized where I was. The guilt settled in like it always did. Maybe my father didn't save me in the dream because he was angry. It was my fault he was missing.

The dream tugged at my mind. My legs were tired and my fingers twitched like I'd actually been swimming, desperate to reach the surface through water that was the orange of flames.

Grandma was a pile of blankets. Her face was hidden but her muffled, scratchy-throat snore sounded like radio static and identified which heap she was. Jessie slept peacefully, like she always did, scrunched into my mother's back for warmth. They looked happy in sleep. Like their dreams were full of pleasant pictures — cakes and chocolate malts and roasted turkey with mashed potatoes. Maybe they saw a house painted yellow with a porch swing for summer nights and a white picket fence all around where red roses lined up in full bloom. I sat there, trying to shake the drowning dream and picture their dreams instead.

All in a rush, I saw myself in a memory, nine years old. Before Jessie. I was wearing my favorite dress, one with clusters of tiny blue forget-me-nots and green leaves scattered on a yellow background. I loved that dress. It had a big collar and pearl buttons all down the front and the fabric was smooth and silky like the edging on a blanket. I used to rub the hem between my thumb and forefinger just to get that feel stuck in my mind. I felt like a lady in that dress and remembered sitting with my knees together so my underwear wouldn't show.

Hunched under my blankets in the green shadows of that preacher's tent and thinking about that dress, I let the memory come.

I was wearing the dress that morning in late June and it'd kept sticking to me. I tugged it down and tucked the hem under my legs. We'd just had a good thunderstorm pass through, and my father and I had been sitting on our porch, huddled together, watching lightning crack the sky and counting after each crash of thunder to figure how many miles up that storm was. Big, fat drops of rain had splashed down, made a few puddles, and passed on in a hurry to get to some thirsty crops up north. The air was washed and fresh, smelling like wet soil and cut grass and honeysuckle. The sun peeked through the clouds and everything turned bright and golden like a fairy had flicked on a magic lamp.

I leaned into my father and he put his arm around me. His white undershirt showed new muscles from lifting big tanks of milk over at Lewis Dairy where he'd worked for the last few weeks, and the hairs on his arms were golden like the fairy light against his dark skin. I loved his smell. Sweat mixed with laundry soap and bleach and the sweet scent of Beech-Nut wintergreen after-dinner mints, the ones he always sucked on when he wasn't drinking whiskey.

I was so happy; I wished I could stop time. Stay there with my father forever in that one spot.

My mother broke the spell. She banged the screen door open with her foot and stomped out carrying a coffee can full of grease, slopping some over the side. She usually buried kitchen grease out back in the garden, so it made me nervous she was coming out front with it.

"You two got all day to waste?" she asked, holding the can in one hand and jabbing the air with the other. "Why aren't you getting ready for work, Ray? You know something I don't know?"

She said it like she did know. She said it like the answer would be bad.

My father looked up at her from his spot on the porch. His green eyes were shiny, and he smiled at my mother in a way I'd seen him do at Christmas when he had a present for her but he knew it wasn't much. I put my hand on his arm and felt a muscle twitch.

"Been fired, Connie," he said. "Couldn't be helped. That

new foreman up from Madison called me thick and said I wouldn't know a cow from a bakery truck. I socked him and he fired me. Didn't even fight back. I meant to tell you. Just spending a little time with the girl here."

My mother poured the grease onto his head. It dripped through his hair, slowly working its way past his eyes and down his nose to his neck and shoulders, bits of bacon and globs of fat sticking to his white undershirt like bugs on flypaper. Some of it splashed onto my favorite dress. The dots landed and I stared, watching them spread.

I flew into a rage. I still don't know where all that mad came from, but it was as if something broke inside me and I couldn't think and I couldn't breathe. I ran at my mother like a wild dog, knocking her back against the house. My arms went crazy and I crashed my fists on her chest, her blocking the blows and trying to get away.

My father grabbed me from behind, his strong arms pinning mine to my side. He said, "Hush now, Elvira. It's all right," in my ear, his voice low and calm.

"You two are exactly alike," my mother screamed. "You're both useless, spoiled babies!"

She threw the coffee can into the yard where it bounced and rolled, then she slammed the screen door so hard I heard a crack and figured it would never close properly again.

I cried. For a long time. My father sat there with me, greasy and sad, stroking my hair and patting my back. My mother didn't come back out.

"I *hate* her," I said.

"Aw, now. No, you don't."

"I do. She's mean and hurtful. I wish I could run away."

"So do I, sometimes," he said.

"You do? You wish you could run away?" I turned to look at him, my eyes blurry from crying and my nose still running. He was staring off at the clearing sky, and at that moment, the sun went behind the last of the clouds, shadows deepened, and I felt a chill. Goosebumps rose on my arms.

"Yes," he said. He put his head in his hands, stared down at his feet. "Sometimes I wish I could sail to the other side of the world."

"Would you take me with you?"

"No, I couldn't do that, Elvira. Your mother needs you here. It's me she doesn't need. I'm a thorn in her side."

"If I were you, I'd do anything to get away from her," I said, jerking my thumb toward the house.

"If you were me, Elvira, you'd love her better. People change. She wasn't always unhappy like she is now. When you were a baby, she sang lullabies when you fussed. I'd sneak up and listen. She hit all the high notes with perfect pitch, pure and clear as rainwater in a crystal glass. Voice like an angel from God."

"She never sings now." I couldn't imagine my mother singing to me. I had no memory of her like that.

"I know. I wish it were still in her, that longing to sing," he said. "It's gone because of me."

"That's not true," I said. He looked so sad. I didn't know how to make him feel better. I put my hand on his arm but he stood, brought his undershirt up to wipe a dab of grease from behind his ear.

"I'm going to town," he said. "Go help your mother. Tell her I'll see her."

I watched him walk, his head down and his shoulders slumped. When he got to the coffee can in the yard, he kicked it and sent it flying. I wanted to run and catch up and grab his hand and never let go. I wanted to shout *Come back, don't leave! I'll be good. I won't talk back and I'll help Mama every day.*

He was only going to town. He'd be back, I told myself.

I heard the squeak of the broken screen door in the middle of the night. Even groggy with sleep, I'd felt the relief of him returning. But at dawn I heard the squeak again and the sound startled me wide-awake. His boots thumped on the front steps. I wrenched my curtain aside and in the gray morning light saw him shift a satchel from one hand to the other, adjust the brim of his hat, and start to walk across the yard. I slid my window up. It scraped from years of paint layers. He stopped and I saw his shoulders tense. I wanted to call out. I could stop him.

But I didn't call out. My voice was frozen in my throat. I didn't call out and he didn't look back. He walked away, me watching at my window until he turned the bend in our drive and was gone.

My father had enlisted. Left a note on the kitchen table saying good-bye to me. Said he'd write when he was on a ship and he'd see me soon.

He never did write.

It was my fault he'd left. I planted the thought of running away in his head and I didn't stop him when I could have.

I never wore that dress again. I still hated dresses. The idea of wearing one turned my stomach.

☙

A wave of sadness washed over me. I had nothing left. No home. No path that led to a secret spot. No father. Only boxes that were stacked in the corner of the tent, my name in block letters on the side of mine. Careful not to wake anyone, I crept on hands and knees and dug to the bottom of my box. Shoved the *Lutheran Ladies' Guild Cookbook* and *A Tree Grows in Brooklyn* aside. Pulled out my treasure sock and untied the knot.

My fingers found the agate first. Even in the dim light I saw the white swirls like whispers of clouds and the black dots in the transparent gray of the stone. Next came the brass button and the scrub jay feather. The tiny pinecone was rough but perfect in its pokiness.

I arranged my treasures in a line and lay the sock beside them. Including the sock, I had five things my father had touched. And his parka. I pulled it from the box and added it to the line. The material rustled and the parka was dangerously close to my mother's feet under the blankets. But I couldn't stop. Six. Six things my father had touched. It was all I had left of him. I felt the trickle of tears before I realized I was crying.

Jessie sighed in her sleep. I wiped my tears away. Enough light seeped through the tent walls now for me to see her profile. Pointy little chin. Turned-up nose with a sprinkle of freckles and pouting lips. Wild curls. *She* was a *part* of him. Why had that not occurred to me before? But knowing a fact doesn't always mean the knowing sinks in to the back of the brain where the understanding part lives.

I heard thumping outside and pans clanging. I figured the preacher was up so I dropped my treasures into the sock and stuffed it into the pocket of my father's parka. Put the bundle back into the box.

Six things my father had touched. He'd never had a chance to touch Jessie, but I had seven treasures just the same. That thought stuck. I had to keep Jessie close to me. When I looked in her green eyes, I saw him.

I wrapped our worn Hudson Bay blanket around my shoulders and as quietly as I could, unzipped the flaps on the tent. It was time that preacher and I had a talk.

Chapter 10

My plan was to come right out with my questions, but I was wary of that preacher. He switched back and forth from smiling to frowning every few minutes. I wasn't sure if he had a lot of thoughts whipping around in his head — some amusing, some serious — and it was hard to keep track, or he had a twitch left over from the accident. Maybe the eye patch was scratchy. Whatever it was, the preacher reminded me of a dog that wags its tail at the same time it's growling and showing teeth. I wasn't sure which thing to trust.

The smell of coffee woke up my nose. Coffee had been rationed for so long my mother had only recently started buying it again. It was a good-day-coming kind of smell. Sugar had been scarce too, expensive on the black market, and even though the war was over and soldiers didn't need as much, the ration was still not lifted. Coffee without sugar tasted like boiled bark. Not that I'd ever actually boiled bark. I'd seen a tin of sugar in with the preacher's things, though. Maybe he'd let me have coffee. So far he'd only smiled when I came out and gone about his business poking the fire with a long stick, waiting for the water to bubble up in our enamel pot.

"You know, stirring a fire is much like writing a sermon," he finally said. "There are tiny sparks of ideas that go around and around in my mind and sometimes they turn into a flame I can use to spread the Word of God. You'll have to forgive me if I seem distracted. I do my best thinking in the morning. Plus, those sparks take some work to ignite."

I'd never seen anyone think so hard it made his face twitch. A fly buzzed my nose. I shooed it. Then I remembered I was mad. I put a frown on and cleared my throat of morning frogs.

"What makes you think she can do it?" I asked.

The preacher glanced at me, raised his eyebrows. Pulled two green ceramic mugs from a box at his feet, then poured the coffee and passed one mug to me with the tin of sugar. "Sorry there's no milk," he said.

I shrugged and swirled my mug to stir in the sugar. Wrapped my hands around it for warmth and put my face near the steam to smell that good-day-coming smell. Except it didn't feel like a good day. I sat as close to the fire as I could tolerate for fear of sparks but as far away from that preacher as possible.

He dragged a log over and sat down. "What makes me think who can do what?" he answered finally, smiling quickly before blowing on his coffee. Then he chuckled, as though I was a young and silly girl. He propped his pointy-toe boots right on the edge of the fire ring. I smelled burning leather.

"You know what I mean," I said, taking a deep breath. "What makes you think Jessie can read minds? Suppose she can't help you with your preaching. Then what? Maybe her hearing my father's song and knowing about your eye surgery and saying those words you said to God was some kind of accident and it will never happen again."

"Oh," he said. "Well, first off, it's not really reading minds. It's a calling. A gift. The words come to her when there's a reason the words need saying. For instance, your sister said a word I hardly ever use — *damnation*. It's a word that shocks, wakes a person up. Gets their attention. Once in a while I have to use it in sermons for that very same reason. Worked, didn't it? And secondly, I believe God is guiding her. Don't you?"

The preacher picked up his stick and stirred the fire again. It was daylight by then but the sun was weak between drifting gray clouds. A squirrel scooted up the trunk of a nearby pine, its bushy tail twitching, and then sat on its haunches on a branch, scolding us. I tugged the Hudson Bay blanket tight under my neck, the scratchy wool making me itch. I must've looked like an old squaw sitting there, the green, red, yellow, and indigo stripes faded and dotted with moth holes. It was warm, though, and something about that blanket wrapped tight made me brave. I was determined to speak my piece. For Jessie's sake.

"No," I said. My knees trembled from nerves. "I don't believe in God. I think you're a fake. You're going to use my sister to make money and that's like stealing. Besides, how can *you* believe in God when he took your eye?"

The preacher touched his patch like I'd reminded him. "He didn't take my eye. He's just giving me some time to see things a little differently. My eye will heal, and I'll be so grateful to him for letting me have them both again, I'll see double the opportunities to spread the Word. Besides, that accident and my prayer of desperation on that day brought me to your mother and Jessie, and I know that was in his plan."

What kind of God would approve a plan that included taking a girl from her home? I tried to make my voice sound disgusted instead of wiggly and weak in my throat. "How *did* you find my mother?" I asked.

"I didn't. She found me. Came to see me at the Sisters of the Divine Savior Hospital while I was recuperating from the surgery. I knew right away your mother had a heart of gold. She sat at my bedside every day, keeping me company, reading the newspaper out loud, pouring a glass of water from the pitcher on the nightstand when I was thirsty. Lifted my spirits. She told me about your sister being a seer. Connie asked me what I thought it might mean, so I told her."

A heart of gold? My mother? So that's where she'd been when I thought she was picking up supplies in town. No wonder she was gone for hours. Since when did my mother do good deeds? And who gave him permission to call her Connie? He should be addressing her as Mrs. Ray Witsil. Out of respect. He was acting a little too familiar.

The preacher hefted another log onto the fire, so green inside it sizzled and smoked. He poured more coffee for both of us. The whistle he'd been working on for Jessie was in the front pocket of his jacket and he pulled it out, running his thumb over the rough cuts. It was starting to take shape, with a groove where the mouthpiece would be, and the opening at the end had a beveled edge.

"Connie decided to offer Jessie's gift to give folks relief from daily troubles," he continued. "Save lost souls from the grief of mourning. Said she's been mourning your father four years and she knew that kind of pain. She said she'd be fine with a small donation. It's not stealing, because people will want to give. It will be their way of saying thank you to Jessie. I don't know if your mother's idea will work, as I suppose it will depend upon Jessie and God, but I don't see any harm in trying. It's not my place to interfere with your mother's plan, and if it's something she feels will help her family, who am I to question that?"

I had to rearrange my thoughts. What was going on? All along I'd thought the preacher had found my mother and swayed her to go along with *his* plan. I'd never stopped to think it could be the other way around.

I also didn't know my mother had been mourning my father's death. If she had, I'd not seen much of that. Something else didn't sit right. How had my mother talked Grandma into going along with the idea? Grandma always said only a fool would take advantage of an easy situation since it was usually an easy situation that came back and bit you in the bottom.

Another thought occurred to me. "What's in it for you?"

The preacher didn't answer right away. He stood up and put his hands in the back pockets of his trousers. Paced back and forth in front of the fire. Then he stopped and looked at me. Frowning. Smiling. Frowning. His eye patch going up and down with each change of expression. I wished someone would get up, wished Grandma or my mother or even Jessie would come out to remind him I was only fourteen and murdering a fourteen-year-old could get him life. But it was him and me and the fire popping and snapping and cracking like rifle shots. I looked at the sky expecting to see buzzards.

But then he laughed. Threw his head back and hooted. I could see up his nose and there was loose skin on the bottom of his chin that jiggled. Finally he held his side as if he had a pain. Dabbed his nose with his sleeve and sniffed.

"Nothing. Nothing at all in it for me," he said. "I don't know why that's funny but it is. I guess I'm so used to giving I forget I could take now and then and it wouldn't bother anybody. Least of all God. Seeing you sitting there thinking I'm all set to rob your family blind just touches my funny bone. Jessie does have a gift. She will help people, and I'm one hundred percent behind the work of God. But the real reason is your mother wants to go to California and I told her I'd help her out. Simple as that. I agreed to take her there after the meeting in St. Paul. That's it. Honest."

That's when I knew my mother had duped the preacher. What I didn't know was why.

Chapter 11

It was late afternoon when we crossed over the St. Croix River into the outskirts of St. Paul, the city on the left, and Minneapolis beyond as far as I could see. The buildings were huge — skyscrapers even — and they looked pretty, made pink from the setting sun and the first lights beginning to twinkle on. The preacher turned down a country lane and we bumped through the gates of the St. Paul fairgrounds. I was excited but nervous now that we had finally arrived. Jessie squealed and pointed and giggled, whipping her head around, trying to see everything at once.

The place buzzed. Dozens of people scurried back and forth setting up tents, pulling out striped awnings on silver Airstream trailers, and smoothing checkered cloths on picnic tables. Suppers cooked in iron barbeque pits, the smells mixing on a light breeze and carrying all through the campground. Small groups gathered in the waning sun, talking and laughing, the men slapping each other's backs. Kids ran around unsupervised, hollering and throwing dirt clods. Someone was picking a guitar and a lady's voice sang "Swing Low, Sweet Chariot," a song I'd heard somewhere once. Maybe on the radio. It was a beautiful song.

The preacher backed into a spot. Before I even hopped out, Jessie and Mabel were over the side of the truck and twirling, stirring up pine needles and dust. I started dumping gear. The preacher held the door and helped my mother down from the truck. She threw her head back and laughed at something he said. I hadn't seen her laugh like that in a long time. She never laughed at anything I said.

On one side of us a family was all set up: a mother and father and two little boys who looked to be about six and eight. Both boys were barefoot, their overalls way above their ankles, the seats too tight and going up their bottoms. I pulled at the seat of my own overalls in sympathy.

They had a green canvas tarp draped over a thick rope tied between two pines and held down by big rocks. I looked inside and saw blankets were spread on the ground. What did they do at night for privacy? The campsite was neat as a pin, though, and a canning jar of yellow wild iris and purple wood violets brightened up the picnic table. I didn't see a car so figured they'd hitchhiked or walked. The revival must be pretty important to them if they'd gone to all that trouble to get here.

The boys watched us unload. They munched on carrots and both their noses twitched like a rabbit's does when it chews. I smiled but they only chewed and stared, the taller of the two drawing lines in the dirt with his big toe.

I unpacked blankets and pillows while Grandma set up

our tent. I watched her. New gray hairs escaped from her bun and she had dark shadows under her eyes. As if she hadn't been sleeping well. None of us were used to camping but maybe it bothered her more.

"Elvira, give me a hand with this tent, for pity's sake. Can't you see I'm struggling here?" she called. I had no choice but to help. Grandma pulled the ropes taut as she banged the stakes into the ground while I held fast to the center pole to keep the whole thing from collapsing. She smelled musty. We were all pretty grubby, but she smelled old. I almost asked her if she was all right, only she was straining to get that tent up and her jaw was set so I kept my mouth shut. Like I'd done all day since the preacher and I talked.

I'd been thinking hard, not that it had helped a bit. I knew there was more going on than I could see. But I couldn't put my finger on it. What was making my mother all fired up to get to California? California had never been mentioned in our house as far as I could remember. Why was Grandma not crabbing and cussing and making her opinions known? She'd been so quiet since we left, it was as if her sharp tongue was glued to the roof of her mouth. It wasn't like her at all.

Only Jessie seemed at ease with everything. Maybe she saw the future and none of it bothered her. Maybe she knew everything would be all right and my mother wasn't a bad person like I was starting to think. If Jessie saw the future, I hoped she saw us all set up in a pretty yellow house like the one I imagined. It had a big porch with red rose bushes blooming along the picket fence and a screen door that would always hang straight because no one would ever kick it. Maybe Jessie already knew I'd have friends. Do well in school. And my mother would turn into the kind of mother who baked and read stories at bedtime all because she was so happy to get to that California sun.

But that wasn't it.

I knew full well things couldn't change that much, no matter how hard I wished. Still, I decided to look for an opportunity to get Jessie alone and ask her. Now that I knew we were going to California, would Jessie tell me why? I could take Mabel away and give the doll back only if Jessie told me what she knew. But that would be mean. Jessie loved Mabel. And Jessie was my seventh treasure. I had to remember that. I had to be nicer.

I pushed my thoughts away and hurried through the work, because I was hoping to get a minute to sneak off by myself and explore. Maybe take *A Tree Grows in Brooklyn* with me. As much as I wanted to read that book, I also was afraid to open it. Once it was over it would be as if I'd lost Mrs. Keller. And finishing the book would give me nothing to look forward to. I knew it was backward thinking.

Mrs. Keller had asked God to watch over us on our journey. She believed in God. Would she have liked this place?

The revival wasn't at all what I expected; I thought people would be solemn and hushed, all dressed in black or brown, thinking about God, heads down as they walked, Bibles tucked under arms, handy in case they needed to look up a passage. Instead, the campground was wild with commotion and laughter.

Kids darted everywhere, chasing each other in games of tag, and it surprised me there were so many of them.

Either they were on summer vacation too or their parents took them out of school for revivals, and if so, no wonder they looked happy. There were lots of little kids. How come all those little kids knew about God but I was fourteen and nobody ever told me anything? But maybe Jessie'd make a friend. I'd start a game of "Mother May I" or "Hide and Go Seek" to get kids interested. I'd do for Jessie what I'd never done for myself.

We didn't have a tablecloth so my mother shook out the old blue-and-yellow quilt and draped it on our picnic table. When I saw it, I longed for Jessie and my bed in our house in Portage, and I wondered if we'd freeze without that quilt.

"Elvira," my mother said. "Get two towels from the box and find the soap. We're having us a hot shower."

I'd never in my life had a shower, always baths in the tub with extra water boiled on the stove since there was never enough hot, so I was pretty excited to hear that news. "A shower? They have showers here?"

"And flush toilets," said my mother, like she'd invented toilets and was offering them as a gift. "Hurry up now and you can wash your hair before we make supper. There should be a bottle of Breck shampoo in with the towels. And get some clean clothes for you and Jessie."

If I didn't do everything my mother asked me to do, the second she asked it, would she notice me?

I dug into my box of clothes and found clean underwear and socks. My hand brushed against my father's parka. When I had a chance, I'd take the treasures out and show them to Jessie. I dug into Jessie's box and got underwear for her. She could use some new socks. Hers were worn and her feet had grown.

Jessie came up and stood on tiptoe so she could see into her box. I'd packed the Tiddledy-Winks, and she pointed at them and said, "Play with me?"

"Maybe later," I said. "After our shower." She smiled and her little white baby teeth reminded me of seashells some-one brought to school once for sharing. I always wanted to own some of those tiny shells to string for a necklace. Did they have those shells in California? A patch of light turned Jessie's brown curls golden, and I thought if she could see that, she'd like it. I felt a swell of love for her right then, and if I ever got any of those shells, I'd make her a necklace too.

Jessie touched my shoulder. "Vira happy?" she asked.

Jessie never did call me Elvira. It wasn't that she couldn't say it, especially now that she talked a mile a minute. She liked Vira better is all. Even I thought of myself as Vira sometimes.

Jessie bounced and wiggled, held Mabel up so the doll could peek over the edge of the clothes boxes. I'd have to find a way to wash Mabel soon. Make her a sundress by cutting up one of our old blouses. Something in a pretty pattern. Poor Mabel wore the same rags every day.

I looked at Jessie. Searched her face. I had thought some-thing in Jessie's green eyes would look different now that I knew she was a seer, but they were the same clear color as always and just as big and bright. I wondered if Jessie looked at me and saw the guilt that was there. I chewed a fingernail. It made me nervous, realizing she might know my thoughts.

"I'm happy enough, I guess," I said, wrapping our underwear in a towel for privacy. I leaned in close and whispered, "Jessie, I know we're going to California. But *why* are we going there? And what's wrong with Grandma? Why is she so quiet? Do you know? Can you tell me?" My heart pounded like I'd done something wrong and was about to get caught.

But Jessie smiled her baby-teeth smile and said, "Grandma's mad. But she has to go. That's all."

"Mad? Grandma's always mad. That's nothing. What do you mean, go?"

I glanced at my mother to make sure she wasn't watching, not that I was ever uppermost in her mind. She was getting pots and pans out, and Grandma was sitting at the picnic table writing something in a notebook I'd never seen before, head bent, shoulders humped, and her arm half across the paper as if she was hiding it from cheaters. The preacher was nowhere to be seen.

"Is there something wrong with her? Is she sick?"

"Grandma has to go. So she sees. That's all," Jessie said again.

I felt panicky, frantic, and I grabbed Jessie's arm. "What do you mean 'that's all'? That's all you'll tell me or that's all you know? Is that why we're going to California? So Grandma can see? See what?"

Jessie clammed up.

"Elvira, let's go, we don't have all night." My mother started to walk off, expecting us to follow without question, which of course we would.

I was shaky. I wondered what Jessie saw that I'd never see. For the thousandth time I wished for a normal sister. One who talked baby talk and played and didn't know the future. Even in my fear, I knew it wasn't fair to Jessie. No little kid should have such a strange life. Neither of us should.

I grabbed our towels and our bar of Ivory soap and took Jessie's hand. She skipped along beside me, kicking up little clouds of dust with her hand-me-down boots. First chance I got, I'd let her go barefoot so her toes could taste the freedom of being a kid in spring.

Chapter 12

The water was warm, not hot, but it spewed out of the showerhead in a forceful stream and it felt good. I scrubbed my hair and body and watched the soap wash down and through the wooden floorboards. The boards had a half-inch gap between them, and I could see gravel below where the soap was piling up and making suds. I figured there was mold down there, and I smelled a mildew smell. The boards felt slimy under my feet like wet moss on a rock in a creek, making me wonder what I was stepping in. But the water was so soothing I decided I didn't care if I got foot rot or some other horrible disease from that shower.

There were only two stalls, and there'd been three women and two girls in front of us, towels draped over their shoulders, so we'd had to wait awhile. But when it was our turn, I was glad there were only two stalls. Just us. My mother and Jessie took one stall, and I got some privacy for a change. If there'd only been one stall, I would have had to listen to my mother talk about the curse.

That's what she called it. The curse. I knew all about monthly miseries but I was a late bloomer and hadn't started all that yet. There'd been girls at school who'd started already; they talked about it in PE as if it were something to brag about. They were the same ones who wore brassieres at twelve, and they giggled and whispered behind their hands whenever I was near. But I was happy to stick to undershirts to cover my tiny bumps. I didn't want to look grown up. Sometimes, when I remembered I had bumps, I'd walk around with my shoulders humped forward to cover up the fact they were there.

My mother would notice and yell, "Shoulders back!" and that would remind her it was time to tell me again about the curse. She loved talking about the curse because it gave her an audience for her own complaints. She always got cramps. Every month. She'd lie on the sofa and moan and twist around on her stomach like that'd help the pains. She'd make me bring her the hot-water bottle and a cup of tea. Red Rose. Had to be Red Rose tea. She said nothing else worked to calm her cramping.

My grandma would roll her eyes and call her a first-class baby and say she never had a cramp in her life that was more than the pinch of a mosquito's bite. Which was also what my grandma called my chest. Mosquito bites. Every time my mother would get all worked up about me becoming a woman and needing a brassiere, my grandma would snort and say they don't make brassieres for mosquito bites, only Band-Aids.

I made myself scarce because their arguments usually turned from my body to some other subject, like my mother's mistake in marrying my father or the lack of money in the house, and sometimes they couldn't remember what started the arguments in the first place, the subjects got so mixed up.

To help them forget about me blooming, as my mother called it, I went around in overalls and baggy sweaters as often as I could and tried to avoid letting my mother see me naked.

My plan was to get out first, before Jessie and my mother finished their shower, even though the water felt so good. It was getting cold anyway. Too bad for the people still in line. I could hear Jessie humming in their stall, so I turned the water off, wrapped my towel around me, and stepped out. Pulled on my clothes even though I wasn't dry. Drips ran down my legs. I stepped on my towel to soak them up, hoping it wouldn't look like I'd peed my overalls when we walked back to camp.

There was a foggy mirror on the wall. I rubbed a spot so I could see and started to comb out my hair. It was full of snarls — this was another of my mother's topics, how I did not take care of my hair properly. It was astonishing how she noticed me the second there was something to criticize. So I hurried, yanking out a few strands as I combed and braided while it was still wet. My hair was too long. I didn't have enough patience for a braid, but my mother would kill me if I ever hacked it off. Maybe I'd do it anyway. Once it was gone, what could she do? I snickered a little as I imagined the look on her face.

Jessie hopped out of the shower, splashing in the puddles

on the floor from the overflow. She shook herself like a dog after a swim and tiny drops of water flew off the ends of her wet curls. Her laugh echoed in the steamy bathroom. I dried her with my damp towel because my mother pushed the curtain back and stepped out with her towel wrapped around her and tucked to hold it in place, and it didn't look like she was giving it up.

"You ladies almost finished in there?" a voice hollered through the partially open door, singsong and pleasant, going up at the end.

My mother frowned and started to snap, "We'll be done when ..." but she remembered she was at a revival with a bunch of godly people and changed her tone to sickly sweet. "Just finishing up. We'll be right out."

She grabbed her clothes, dabbed at herself with the towel, then turned to us and said, "Hurry up, girls." Like we'd been holding her up.

I ran the comb through Jessie's hair, trying to hurry without yanking. Made her stand still while I helped her get dressed. Stuffed my clean socks into my pocket and slipped on my sneakers, wet feet squishing. We trooped out. My mother held the door and smiled at the lady and her daughter, who were next. The lady smiled back as though my mother was always pleasant and might be someone to be friends with. Fat chance.

The daughter looked at Jessie and said to me, "Cute kid. She your sister?"

"Yeah," I answered, pushing Jessie gently to keep her moving since my mother was already way ahead and I wasn't real sure yet how to get back through the winding campground and find our spot.

But Jessie decided it was another opportunity for her to make my life even more difficult.

"Don't ride double," she said, smiling sweetly up at the girl who wasn't all that much taller than Jessie, but must have been older, seven or eight, and skinny as a stick.

The girl's jaw dropped. She had on a white blouse with puffy short sleeves and her face was about the same color, she was so surprised.

"What?" she asked, looking at me. "Is she touched in the head? What's she talking about, 'don't ride double'?"

"Don't ride double," Jessie said again.

We were standing just outside the door to the shower building and that girl's mother had gone in already, but there was a long line of women and girls listening to every word. I wished my own mother would turn around and notice we were not behind her anymore and call us to catch up quick, so I could grab Jessie and say, "Sorry, we gotta scram," and I wouldn't have to answer the girl's question. But my mother kept walking.

"Gee, I'm not sure what she's talking about," I stammered, nudging Jessie again to get her going. "She's pretty little and she likes to joke around. Heh. Heh." My fake laughs never sounded real like some people's fake laughs. What was Jessie doing? This was not a good way to make a friend. I had to get us out of there.

Jessie's eyes rolled back, her body went rigid, and the color drained from her cheeks. "Don't ride double," Jessie said again. I took her hand. Squeezed it. Tried to get her to move. But her feet were planted.

It would have been better if the girl teased us or poked fun at Jessie and we could have turned our backs and moved on with dignity, ignoring her. Instead, the girl got this look of pain on her face as if she'd seen a dead kitten on the road and she bent a little, her blonde hair swinging down her back.

"I'm sorry you're troubled," she said to Jessie. "God will help you."

And I about threw up. Not because it was so bad she was churchy instead of teasing, but because suddenly I hated that someone felt sorry for Jessie like that. Thinking she was crazy and needing the help of God to fix her twisted mind. My stomach jumped up and traded places with my heart, both thumping around in my body like running feet. I could taste sour in my mouth like throw up was on its way. I was about to grab the girl's hair and yank it to teach her a lesson about making assumptions when Jessie grabbed the back of my overalls and yanked me instead.

Jessie was strong. I fell backward and landed in the dust, and some of it stuck to my damp bottom and my rolled cuffs.

"Sorry," Jessie whispered and showed her seashell baby teeth.

Some ladies helped me up, brushing the dust off, clicking their tongues *tsk, tsk, tsk* the entire time and shaking their heads at the tragedy of simpleminded children. But the commotion was enough to get us on our way. Plus, my mother was gone from sight. Jessie called one more time, "Don't ride double," and a few of those ladies and a lot of the kids smiled in sympathy and put their hands over their hearts.

I wanted to shout, "She's not simpleminded and she's not crazy! My sister is a seer." I wanted to prove it to them.

As much as I didn't want a seer for a sister, they had no right to judge her. I could think Jessie was strange but they couldn't. We didn't need their sympathy. And if there was a God and all these people believed in him so much, why didn't he teach them all a lesson? Make them change their tune.

"Don't look back," I said, wishing we could run.

"I know," said Jessie. She skipped along beside me, same as always, back to her regular self.

Chapter 13

In the dark, all the camps looked the same — Coleman lanterns on the tables and campfires flickering, shadows dancing — but we finally found ours by following the preacher's voice. He was reading out loud from the Bible, and his tone for reading was even deeper than his talking voice.

"And here's one of my personal favorites," he was saying. There was a small crowd gathered at his feet, sitting on blankets on the ground. People gazed at him as if they didn't want to miss a word. I noticed the two little boys from the camp next door standing off in the protection of the pines, their eyes bright spots in their faces like wild animals' eyes in moonlight.

My mother saw us creeping up and said, "What took you so long?"

Some mothers would have had a search party out, we'd

been gone so long; not her though. I was surprised she'd even noticed. She only missed me when something needed doing. Sure enough, she handed me potatoes to peel.

"Throw the peel on the fire when you're done," she said. "Then find the plates." My mother took a moment to glance my direction. "Elvira, you're dirty. Can't you stay clean five minutes?"

She scowled and shook her head, put her hands on her hips. She'd painted her nails bright red while we'd been gone, and I wondered how that would sit with the preacher and all the other revival folks. Someplace I'd heard painted finger-nails were against church rules. Like dancing and drinking. I'd heard that too. I was embarrassed for my mother, pictur-ing her shunned because her nails were red like a floozy's.

"Sorry," I said. "The paths are dusty." I didn't feel like arguing, and I wasn't about to tell her what Jessie had said back at the showers. What would be the point? It probably didn't mean anything anyway.

I peeled and Jessie skipped back and forth from my peel pile to the fire, dumping the bits, watching them sizzle and curl, captivated by the flames and the spiral of smoke car-rying sparks to the sky. It seemed we were the last ones in the campground to eat.

Grandma stirred a pot of something. She was awfully quiet. I still wasn't used to that.

The preacher read, "'... Surely goodness and mercy shall follow me all the days of my life: and I will dwell in the house of the Lord forever.' Psalm twenty-three." And then he said, "His house may be the shelter of fragrant boughs, or your own yard where children play, or the back of my old truck, so long as he is in your thoughts."

I didn't know what the heck he was talking about, but the back of the preacher's truck was not like any house I'd ever wanted, and I was already getting sick of the tent. But then it occurred to me he meant you could believe in God anywhere, not just in some old stuffy church. You could pray and read the Bible in the middle of a campground and it was all a fine thing to do. God apparently didn't mind where you were as long as you believed. It sounded easy. Only I wasn't sure I could believe. A lot of it didn't make sense.

I stood up to carry the potatoes to the pot of boiling water.

A woman screamed.

It was chilling and loud, like the echoes back home but trailing off into the kind of cry that comes with bad pain. Everybody on the blankets jumped up, whipped their heads back and forth as if the screamer would drop from the sky. Grandma and my mother stopped what they were doing.

Jessie slipped her hand in mine. It was warm. So small and soft.

People grabbed lanterns and flashlights against the darkness and ran toward the sound.

But it wasn't the scream that I knew would stick in my mind for years to come; it was the sound of all those running feet, crunching on gravel and snapping twigs, and the puffing, wheezing, heavy breathing of people afraid.

I knew she was dead the second I saw her, a picture of the little girl that would never leave me.

Blood pooled on the ground next to her head and her white puffy-sleeved blouse was spattered with dots of red.

Lanterns flickered as people held them high and I thought she'd moved. No. She was dead. The girl's mother sobbed, her fingers twisting the girl's long blonde hair a few strands at a time, as if fixing that hair would fix her head too. People pulled at the mother, trying to move her away from the body, but she slumped down beside her daughter, unwilling to leave. Folks prayed, soft and low. Women cried. The preacher knelt beside the girl's mother and whispered into her ear. I couldn't hear what he was saying but the mother sat up and crumpled into him, a rag doll.

Why hadn't I done something? I felt dizzy. Sick to my stomach. I'd wanted to prove my sister was a seer, not simple-minded. I'd wished for God to teach them all a lesson. I hadn't meant this. How could God let that girl die?

The bicycle was crooked and broken, the wheel bent in half and jammed up against the boulder that caused the accident. The boy who'd packed her on the handlebars sat in the dirt, sobbing. A man tried to examine his wounds. The boy pushed him away.

I tightened my grip on Jessie's hand. I felt her trembling. I should've followed that girl around to stop this terrible thing from happening.

Jessie whispered to the air, "Don't ride double. Sorry, little girl."

My mother found us in the crowd. She leaned down and her breath tickled my ear, making me shiver. "What did Jessie say?" she asked in a quiet voice so no one would hear.

But everyone did hear. People turned around, pointing, whispering. Like they used to do back home when they gossiped about my father and his drinking. I recognized some of the women who'd helped me up and brushed the dust off my overalls. But this time they looked at Jessie with awe instead of sympathy. They were shocked but fascinated. Like moths that know they'll burn but flicker over flames anyway.

One tear trickled down Jessie's cheek, but she didn't make a sound. Was it really her fault? The girl ignored the warning. Jessie told her not to ride double. I had dragged Jessie away. If I hadn't done that, would Jessie have followed the little girl and saved her? As she'd saved my mother from a bad cut by switching the knives that time in our kitchen back home? And why would God let the girl ride double anyway? If God was real, did he make mistakes?

I wished we could leave. Just Jessie and me. Hide somewhere until all this passed. I wished that God was real so I could ask him for the favor of taking Jessie's seeing capabilities and giving them to someone else.

But Grandma always said, "You can't turn back the clock."

So right when I was getting used to the idea of the revival, we had to have a funeral instead.

Chapter 14

Word travels fast in a campground. Thanks to my mother and her flapping lips, in the short time between the girl's death and morning, everyone knew Jessie would be offering her services for a small donation. When I woke up, there was a line of people worming around our picnic table, waiting to get started.

The crowd seemed uneasy. Men shifted from foot to foot, silent, with arms folded and heads to the ground. Women chattered in clusters, but they kept their voices low as though talking loudly would disturb Jessie's concentration. Or bring another death. I couldn't shake that guilt. I wanted to talk to someone about it. Anyone. But who would listen to me? The campground was keeping us at arm's length, and my mother and Jessie were holed up in the preacher's tent.

I hated my mother's prophesying scheme. The whole

thing felt wrong. Disgraceful. How could the preacher believe it was God's plan? Plus, it was embarrassing having a mother who would use her own child to make money. I wanted to grab Jessie and run. But even if I'd had somewhere to run to, I couldn't have grabbed her. My mother was guarding her like a hawk.

The tent flap had been opened, and Jessie's face peeked out above a card table someone had loaned. Mabel lay on the floor. Jessie sat on a canvas camp stool, and her feet didn't even reach the floor, she was so little. She swung her legs back and forth. Jessie didn't look disturbed. She looked amused, like she was enjoying all the attention, but I figured that was because she didn't really know what was expected of her.

I wished she'd never been born.

Right away I was sorry for that thought. It wasn't her fault she'd been born a seer. It wasn't her fault people would be asking all kinds of questions, expecting her to know the answers or predict their future. Like knowing the future would give them the right to change it. The preacher had said seeing was a gift from God, but how did he know? It seemed more of a curse to me. You'd think God would want to be the only one who could see things. Maybe that's why the people in the line looked embarrassed. They felt guilty going against God as though his advice wasn't enough. Grandma always said, "I don't believe in anything that I can't see right in front of my face." Jessie was right here, flesh and blood. God was invisible. Maybe that was it. People believed what they saw.

My mother had positioned an apple crate outside the tent. On it was a cooking pot, and propped above was a sign that said "DONATIONS" in big, black letters on a cardboard flap torn from a box. She stood at the entrance to the tent, stiff and serious, like a soldier. Or Scrooge, waiting to count her money. Money obtained by taking advantage of someone else.

I'd promised to protect Jessie. I had to figure out some way to get in that tent in case she needed me to snatch her away from all those vultures. But at that moment all I could think of was getting to the bathroom. The problem with camping is you have to hold it when you get up in the morning until after you're dressed, and then you have to walk all the way to the bathroom, and chances are when you get there, you'll have to stand in line. But today, maybe not, since it seemed the entire campground was in line to see Jessie instead.

I was about to sneak off before my mother saw me, but Grandma's voice rattled my teeth. "Elvira," she said sharply, like I'd been ignoring her. "Come over here this minute."

I hadn't even seen her. She was hunched in the back of the preacher's truck, leaning on a bed pillow up against the cab, out of the view of the line. I sucked my stomach in to hold back what I needed to hold back and walked over to the truck. The morning air was cool and a mist hung low, making my hair and face feel damp, which didn't help my bathroom situation at all.

Grandma handed me a piece of lined paper folded into a small, neat square. "Give this to your mother," she said.

Not a good sign. It meant they weren't speaking. Sometimes when they argued, they got so mad they wouldn't talk to each other, but they were both so stubborn neither could stand not having the last word. So they wrote notes instead. This usually went on for days. I was always the delivery girl. Grandma would write the first note, then I'd have to wait while my mother scribbled a response. She'd say, "Give this to your grandmother." Even if Grandma was five feet away and could hear every word. They both watched me when I delivered the notes to make sure I didn't read what they'd written.

I groaned. "Can I go to the bathroom first?"

Grandma snorted, which was actually a good thing given she'd been quiet for days. I'd been wondering when she'd get back to her grouchy old self.

"Most of us don't sleep the day away," she said. "If you'd get up earlier, it wouldn't be such an emergency. You're just like your mother, waiting until the last minute for everything, then making a big dramatic production out of the simplest problems."

I took the note over to my mother. She ignored me and ushered a woman into the tent to sit with Jessie. She zipped up the flap for privacy, yanking it. My mother was the only one in the world who could slam a tent door. She quickly snapped back to wooden-soldier position, arms folded.

I held the note up in front of her nose.

"Stop it, Elvira," she said. "Go find something to do."

"It's a note from Grandma," I said, knowing full well it would set her off but also knowing she couldn't make a big fuss in front of all those people. Her nostrils flared and her cheeks turned red. A vein throbbed in her neck and lines formed like chicken tracks between her eyebrows.

"Get me paper and a pencil," she said, just like I'd known she would.

Grandma wouldn't give up any of her notepaper or loan her ballpoint pen so I rummaged in our tent and tore off a chunk of paper sack. Found a stub of pencil. While my mother was writing I crossed my legs. Tried not to wiggle, straining at the same time to hear what was going on in the tent.

The lady in there was crying. "Please," she said, in a begging sort of way, the word drawn out. I heard Jessie answer, "No, can't," and the lady said, "Please," again.

Jessie said, "Not for you to know." Whatever it was the lady wanted, she wasn't going to get it. Good. Serves her right. Serves my mother right too, for putting Jessie on display in the first place.

The lady came out wiping her eyes with a hanky. She passed up the donation pot, shooting my mother a dirty look. Stalked out of our campsite, dust puffing up around her feet. My mother paid no attention. She was too busy writing her note.

The next person, a man this time, ducked into the tent and zipped the flap himself. I then heard a snap. My mother broke the point on the pencil, she'd been pressing so hard. She wadded up the brown paper and slammed it into my hand.

"Give this to your grandmother," she said, again like I'd known she would. I almost said the words myself.

The man had a loud voice. "Can you tell me where she is?"

"No," Jessie said and started to hum a tune.

The man asked, "Why not?"

Jessie didn't respond. Maybe she shook her head but I didn't hear another word. The man came out, his face all twisted as if he was embarrassed for being suckered in like that. I wondered who it was he wanted to find. He passed up the donation pot too, not even dropping in a penny. At that rate, my mother wasn't going to make much money. No matter how much we needed money, that prospect made me happy.

I had to get out of there. My mother wasn't going to let me rescue Jessie. Not that I had to at the moment. My sister seemed to be holding her own. May as well give up and check on her later. I skipped the few feet to the preacher's truck, tossed the wad of paper at Grandma, and made a beeline for the bathroom.

"Come right back, you hear?" she called.

But I kept running.

And I wasn't coming right back.

Chapter 15

I took my time washing my hands in the chipped por-
celain sink, staring in the hazy mirror and wishing I
didn't have so many freckles. I had a pimple on the inside
of my nose. It was a stupid place for a pimple. Not that there
ever is a good place, but the inside of a nose is a pretty difficult spot to put a warm compress, something my mother
made me do when I broke out.

"A clear complexion is important, Elvira," she always
said. "If you want boys to notice you, think about your
appearance, for once." I didn't care if boys noticed me.
There were never any boys worth knowing in Portage, and
even if there were, none of them would take an interest in
someone like me.

I flapped my hands dry since I forgot to bring a towel
and poked stray hairs back into my braid, knowing I should
take it out and redo the whole thing. I'd rather hack it off.

I was sick of looking like a country bumpkin, boys aside. If I cut it, I could crimp it in waves the way Mrs. Keller wore her hair. What was she doing right this minute? Had she thought about me since I left? I could kick myself for not taking the time to dig *A Tree Grows in Brooklyn* out of my box before I ran off to the bathroom. I was still afraid to finish it, but I'd read the first line, and it sucked me right in. "*Serene was a word you could put to Brooklyn, New York.*" *Serene* was not a word you could put to me.

A tattered war poster of Uncle Sam was tacked to the outside wall of the bathroom, and he did not look serene at all. I hadn't noticed the poster before. But I'd seen a hundred of them on buildings and stores in Portage, although most of the posters had been gone for ages. People with sons or husbands in the war had even put them up in the windows of their houses. Ugly, old codger in a red, white, and blue top hat, one fat finger pointing in a threatening way. "Uncle Sam Wants You." As if one man refusing to enlist could bring down a country.

I hated the war. It took my father. But it wasn't Uncle Sam's fault.

The campground was quiet. It was still chilly and I smelled rain coming. I turned the opposite direction from where we were camped and followed a different path, pine needles crunching under my sneakers. A dog barked way off. For years I'd begged for a dog. Even though we'd always lived out in the middle of nowhere with plenty of room for a dog to run, my mother had never let me have one. I wasn't sure why. Maybe my mother thought that a dog would argue with her like Grandma did.

What was making Grandma mad at her this time? It

could be anything, but it must have something to do with my mother's decision to travel with the preacher. It was enough for me. Maybe I'd stop speaking to her too. Start passing notes instead.

I remembered the first time they'd passed the notes, the first time the silence fell on the house. The beginning of my job running back and forth like a puppet. It was when my mother's stomach was just getting big with Jessie but she could still fit in regular dresses and wasn't yet wearing the old shirts my father left behind. Grandma had come to stay until he was back from the war.

It was a cold, overcast, snow-in-the-air kind of day.

It was the day of the Western Union man.

He came up, cutting across the grass, and stood on the porch in his Western Union uniform, all pressed and perfect with creases like a paper fold down the middle of his trousers. His black hair was slick and trimmed close around the ears, and the top of his head was covered by a peaked cap. He held an envelope and a clipboard. He'd knocked with the clipboard. I could tell by the sound, a sharp smack on the thick wood of the front door.

I answered.

"Is this the Witsil residence?" he asked, checking his list of names.

"Yes," I said, and I liked the sound of the words — Witsil residence — like we were fancy folks.

"Is there a Mrs. Ray Witsil here, first name Constance?" he asked. He held an envelope by two fingers as if it had been dipped in poison.

And suddenly I was afraid. My knees shook. Cold shivers rippled up and down my arms.

"Mama!" I screamed and slammed the door in his face. I knew. I ran to my room and hid in the closet. I knew. I'd made my father leave and now he wasn't coming back.

I must've fallen asleep. It was dark when I heard the crying. It went on and on. Sobs so big they made my chest hurt like I'd been crying too. I crept down the hall and saw Grandma sitting with my mother on the floor in the living room. My mother was crumpled over, her face in her hands and her stomach sticking out. She looked as though someone had wadded her up and thrown her there.

"What will I do?" she wailed. The front of her dress was sopping wet, darker blue than the rest. Her nose was running in a steady stream. Grandma handed her a tissue but my mother didn't blow.

"You'll get over it. Living without that good-for-nothing husband will be a blessing in the end," said Grandma. "Ray never did one thing to make you proud. You could never depend on him. He couldn't hold a job and he couldn't hold his whiskey. You're above him, like I was with your father. Take it from me; it was easier living without him than it was living with him. You'll see. Good riddance if you ask me."

"Don't you ever compare Ray with my father!" screamed my mother. "Ray never laid a hand on me. Not once. Ray never lost his mind from drink like the man you married. And he didn't go away on purpose, leaving his wife and baby behind."

"Oh no? That's exactly what Ray did when he enlisted, Connie. How can you be so stupid?"

And my mother smacked Grandma. Red finger marks appeared on the side of her face.

For days they passed notes. I ran back and forth, back and forth. Neither of them explained but I knew the Western Union man had brought a letter that said my father was dead. Later, when I stole it from my mother's dresser drawer and read it out back under the porch with the spiders and the earthworms and the smell of old rotting wood from the broken step, I saw where it said *missing in action* but I knew that meant gone. I'd told him to run away. He didn't leave my mother on purpose. Grandma was wrong. It was my fault he'd enlisted.

While walking on that campground path with the patches of light breaking through the deep green of the pines, the silence broken only by the soft buzz of insects and the distant calls of crows, I realized that, just like me, my mother had loved my father. She must've seen some good in him despite what Grandma tried to make her believe. My mother cried long and hard the day of the Western Union man. She'd mourned my father. Like the preacher said, she knew that kind of pain.

My mother moved us out in the middle of nowhere to keep an eye on my father, but thanks to me, he slipped off anyway. Why did he listen? He should've found a new job, poured out his whiskey once and for all, and been the father I needed. Sometimes it seemed like he got the easy way out, leaving me behind with all these questions and no one to ask.

I arrived at a fork in the path. A wooden marker stuck out of the ground with "Campsites 46 – 58" and an arrow painted on it. I'd come the wrong way but a wonderful smell reached my nose. I should've been checking on Jessie but I couldn't turn back. I followed the smell.

A lady squatted over a campfire. She used a wooden spoon to flip some messy slop with brown lumps and green shreds like strips of wilted leaves in an iron skillet. How could something that smelled so good look that awful? My stomach growled so loud I thought she'd hear, and she did look up and smile.

"You want some, yes?" she asked.

She had an accent I'd never heard and it sounded like "you vant soom, yaw?" Her cheeks were fat and rosy like a carnival clown's cheeks and when she smiled they got fatter. Her body was so big she wore a skirt that ballooned, reaching to thick ankles, and a huge man's shirt with the cuffs rolled so her wrists would fit through. The front buttons strained. Grandma would've said, "Nothing wasted on that one."

"No. Thanks. I have to get back." I did want some, though. I was starving.

"You that girl's sister."

She didn't ask it. She stirred, not looking at me. I backed up a step.

"Poor little dear," she said as she slopped a pile of food onto a tin plate and handed it to me.

"What is it?" I didn't want to be rude, but I didn't want to eat gopher's feet or squirrel stew either.

She laughed. "It is sausage," she said. "You will like. In Germany, we eat sausage all the time. That is why we fat. I make with cabbage and onion and some bacon, little salt, pepper. It is good. Go ahead. Eat."

I took the plate and copied the way she scooped up a bite with a slice of bread. It was delicious. Spicy.

The only Germans I'd ever seen were German Lutherans back home in Portage, watching them by the school bus stop as they came and went from St. John's. But they didn't have accents; they were all born in Wisconsin. And the only Lutheran I really ever met was the white-haired lady we bought the *Lutheran Ladies' Guild Cookbook* from, the one who said "Peace be with you" to my mother. So I figured Lutherans might be all right but Germans I wasn't so sure about. This lady was a real German. A German like the ones our men had been fighting in the war. I was a little afraid of her. Everyone knew the bad things Germans had done and stories were still coming out about how they'd treated the Jews over in Europe.

"Not all Germans bad," she said, like she was reading my mind.

"I didn't say that," I said. But I had thought it. I swallowed a lump of sausage and wished I had a drink to wash it down.

The lady sopped up grease with her last bit of bread and popped it into her mouth, licking her fingers one by one.

"I can tell from face you scared of Germans," she said. "Some Germans help Jews get out. Not all bad. I ashamed of bad Germans. What they do to Jews … how you say?"

"Horrible?"

"Yes, horrible. God cries. Good Germans help, not all bad. But not enough good Germans. Most look other way. God cries now."

If God was crying now, how come he let all those Jews

die in the first place? That didn't make sense. Did God cry when he took my father?

The German lady smiled at me. A toothy smile like a horse about to bite. But I liked her. I liked this lady with big cheeks and strange food, and I didn't know why but I thought she liked me too.

"Why is my sister a poor little dear?" I set my plate on the ground beside me. Leaned back against a pine tree, my overalls tight across my full stomach.

She took a long time to answer. She seemed to be holding her breath. Her fat cheeks puffed out even more. When she finally released the breath she sucked her bottom lip.

"She is poor little dear because she must do hard things. Children should play. Go to school and laugh with friends. But no, poor little dear will not have that. Instead, poor little dear sees too much sadness."

"How do you know that? How do you know Jessie sees too much sadness?"

"I know because I too am seer. I was little girl saw too much horrible. Now I'm grown woman sees too much horrible."

How could that be? Before Jessie, I'd only had half an idea of what a seer was — someone who traveled with the circus or the ghost in Dickens' *A Christmas Carol* who wore a flowing cape and beard and told stories of the past, present, and future. I never expected to meet a real one, let alone two. This woman didn't look like any seer I'd ever imagined. She wore no turban like fortune-tellers usually did. No gold bangles clanked at her wrist, and no necklaces bunched around her fat neck. She wasn't wearing velvet robes that floated when she walked. Instead the hem of her old skirt dragged on the ground collecting dust. She looked like a hobo.

But Jessie didn't look like a seer either. She looked like a normal little girl.

I had so many questions. I wanted to ask her why some people could see and others couldn't. Would Jessie always know what was coming or would she grow out of it, lose some of the touch? Did the ability come from God or someplace else? I wanted to know what this lady had seen so I could warn Jessie in case the same was coming up for her. What was seeing like? Did it hurt like a headache?

"I not going tell you," she said. "I not going tell you what poor little dear life be like. Sometimes cannot change what is to come. Sometimes can. I know this. From hard way. I come seven years ago to America on big boat with husband and two fine boys. My sons. On boat all get bad sick, all die of bad sick. I alone. No money. Stay by self in America. In Germany, before we get on boat, I knew this going to happen."

She shifted her bulk, struggled to her feet, and waddled closer. Her eyes were pale blue and they filled with tears. She pointed to herself, poking hard at her chest.

"I knew they going to die." Her voice was a whisper now, raspy with the pain of remembering.

I felt my eyes fill.

"I knew," she said again. "I try to warn them. Husband not listen, want America so bad. We come anyway. Now, no family. No home. I follow every day these church believers town to town. Meeting to meeting. Thinking maybe God forgive me. Maybe God tell me why this have to happen. But no use. I not forgive myself." The German lady swayed with her bulk as she bent to gather our plates and her cooking pot. I started to help her but she waved me off.

"You must do what poor little dear say. She leading you. You follow. She leading Mother and Grandma too. Listen to everything poor little dear say. You go now."

Then she reached into a pocket and pulled out a clean, white handkerchief with delicate lace edges. Handed it to me.

"Here. Take this. Remember what I tell you when you see hanky. White hanky mean truth. You listen to everything poor little dear say. She telling truth."

A wind came up, stirring ash in her campfire, and for a second the coals glowed red. She turned her back and waddled to an old, beat-up Ford parked under the pines. The car was packed to the roof with boxes and folded blankets. Probably everything she owned. She tossed the pans through an open window, heaved into the driver's seat, and shut the door. The engine roared to life.

"Wait," I called, running after the cloud of dust. I didn't even know her name.

She didn't stop. I looked for initials on the handkerchief but there were none. I folded it, fingering the lace. How had she kept it clean when the rest of her was so dirty and disorderly?

I felt sick to my stomach. That German lady couldn't save her husband and sons. She knew what was going to happen and she hadn't done enough. No wonder she never forgave herself.

Jessie had warned the little girl not to ride double, and the little girl died. What was the point of seeing if everyone died anyway? I headed back toward our camp, dragging my feet, thinking about everything the German lady said.

I didn't understand.

I put the handkerchief in my pocket. Truth. A white hanky means truth. She said Jessie was leading us. What was she leading us to? What did the German lady mean I must listen?

But I knew I would listen.

I knew that whatever Jessie said to do, I'd do.

Chapter 16

W here have you been? Wandering off when there's work to be done. That behavior won't do, Elvira."

I *had* been gone a long time. My mother and the preacher sat at the picnic table, both on the same bench, shoulders touching. She'd pinned her hair in a French knot. Tendrils escaped, curling from the humidity in the air. It still smelled like rain and gray clouds tumbled across the sky, blocking the feeble afternoon sun. I heard the rat-a-tat-tat of a woodpecker high above where the wind was picking up, pine branches swaying like graceful dancers.

My mother had put the preacher to work peeling potatoes. It seemed that's all we had left to eat. I hoped I could get out of eating. I was still full from my meal with the German lady.

"Sorry," I said. "I got lost." I wasn't going to tell her where I'd been. Not that it mattered, since she didn't ask.

The preacher waved his peeling knife in greeting. He'd removed the eye patch but his eye wasn't completely healed. He looked like a raccoon, greenish bruises under and above his eye. The white was bloodshot. He looked less like a gangster without the patch. Friendlier.

The line was gone. So were Jessie and Grandma. The donation pot was the potato pot now, half full of water. I wondered if Jessie'd seen sadness like the German lady said she would. Our neighbors were sitting at their picnic table, heads bent and hands folded, saying grace before an early supper. The two little boys didn't look my way. They must be keeping to themselves since we were so strange.

"Where's Jessie?" I asked my mother.

"I'm going to lie down," she said in response.

The preacher raised his eyebrows and watched my mother disappear into our tent and zip the flap. He frowned and then the corners of his mouth curled in a smile. I remembered that meant he was thinking hard. Or praying maybe. He looked up and I followed his gaze but didn't see anything except a hawk gliding gracefully over the pines.

"Your mother is worn out. A rest will do her good," he said, turning to me. "Quite a crowd around here earlier. Took a lot out of her."

He was sticking up for my mother. Making excuses for her rudeness. I'd never get away with walking off and not answering a question. She never followed her own rules. She wouldn't need a rest if she hadn't flaunted Jessie in the first place. Did the preacher think of that?

"She certainly is a beautiful woman." He blushed. Even his ears turned red.

"Judging by the expression on your face, I probably shouldn't have said that. She is, though. Quite becoming. You look a lot like her."

I realized my mouth was hanging open. I clamped my jaw shut and felt my teeth clack together. The last person in the world I wanted to resemble was my mother. For a second I was so stuck on that idea, it didn't register the preacher had paid my mother a compliment. He thought she was beautiful. Were preachers even supposed to say those things? I looked down, scuffed the dirt.

"Where are Jessie and my grandma?"

He seemed relieved I'd changed the subject. "Your grandma went for a walk and Jessie insisted on going with her," said the preacher. "There's no stopping that young one when her mind's made up. You've got to admire that."

That was a nice thing for the preacher to say about Jessie even though *stubborn* was the word we used to describe her. But I didn't want Jessie out of my sight. Anything could happen. The German lady said I should do everything Jessie said to do. What if Jessie said something I wasn't there to hear? When Jessie returned I'd dig into Grandma's scraps and make Mabel a dress. That would keep her close. I almost laughed when I remembered how she stuck to me like glue back home in Portage. Now it was the other way around.

"Maybe I should go look for them," I said, standing up.

"I'm sure they're fine. They've only been gone a few minutes. Want to help me peel?"

I wasn't sure how to get out of peeling so I sat on the bench next to the preacher. He handed me the paring knife and pulled out a pocketknife, unfolding the blade with a click. "Let's see if I can peel this potato in one long strip," he said. "I always wanted to try that."

I'd always wanted to try that too. It surprised me we had that silly thing in common. We peeled in silence but I got the feeling we were secretly racing each other, trying to win by peeling the longest strip in the fastest time.

The preacher broke the silence. "I've been hoping to ask you something. Your mother said you're a good reader. I was wondering if you'd read through the sermon I've written for tomorrow's funeral. Would you mind?"

"What funeral?" I asked, without thinking. I was so amazed my mother had said something good about me, I forgot about the little girl who'd died. "Oh, right. Sorry. I guess I could read it for you." I felt the weight of the girl's death settle in my stomach.

"Ha! Look at that. Bet this one's longer than yours," he said, holding up a strip of peel as if he'd caught the biggest fish.

I couldn't help but laugh. He looked so proud of that peel. "I guess you win," I said. But suddenly, I was angry. I threw my peel to the ground. "Why did God let that girl die? Jessie tried to warn her."

The preacher stopped peeling. Stared off, not looking at me. "I don't know. I wish I had that answer. I know it bothers you. The little girl dying and having a sister who knew it was going to happen. It's a hard thing to carry. But it wasn't Jessie's fault. And it wasn't yours. Don't take the blame, Elvira."

I felt tears coming. I swallowed to hold them back. No one ever cared how I felt about anything. I'd kept my thoughts and feelings inside for so long they were all mixed up, tumbling around in my stomach, heavy like rocks, making my chest tight with little pains shooting through my heart. Everything bothered me. The girl's death. Having a sister who knew too much. It bothered me that Grandma and my mother weren't speaking to each other. I had no home. I didn't know why we were going to California. My father was gone. That *was* my fault. There was no one to blame but *me* for that. I hated my whole stupid life. I felt empty and exhausted.

But what I said was, "Why did you have to drag us to this dumb revival? We never even went to church before. You could've told my mother no. You could've told her it was a selfish idea to traipse around the country showing off her kid. It isn't fair."

And then I did cry. The preacher patted my hand.

"You don't want to share Jessie, do you?"

I sniffed. How did he get that out of what I'd said? But I realized it was true. I was so used to taking care of Jessie it was like she belonged to me. She was my seventh treasure. I didn't want to share her.

"You're lonely," the preacher said. He leaned closer and patted my hand again. "Make a friend in God, Elvira. He'll fill that empty place. I don't think there's anyone that little girl loves more than she loves you. But there's a reason for all this pain you feel. I think you're carrying a burden too heavy for your shoulders. I don't know what it is, but I know God has a reason for you to carry it. Just like I know he has a reason for giving Jessie the gift. It'll come clear. Pray about it."

"I don't know how to pray. I never did it." If God were real, why would he listen to me?

"Do you ever wish on a star?"

It seemed silly to admit it. "Yes," I said. "Sometimes."

"Wishing on a star is a little bit like praying. Imagine that your star is the place where God lives, way up there in that big, beautiful expanse of sky. Ask a question. Ask for a clear path to the answer. He is more powerful than we can ever understand, Elvira. You've just got to give him a chance."

Even though I didn't completely believe what the preacher was telling me, suddenly I felt better, lighter, as if the rocks in my stomach had turned to dust. I wanted to tell the preacher everything — how I'd made my father leave, and if I hadn't planted that thought of running away in his mind, he'd be here with us today; how I could have stopped him that morning but didn't have the words; that my father drank too much whiskey but he'd also been decent, kind, funny, and smart, and nobody but me remembered that.

The preacher pulled folded papers from his inside jacket pocket. Handed the sermon to me.

"I'd appreciate your opinion. I'll have time to make changes tonight. Funeral's at nine o'clock tomorrow morning."

"We never had a funeral for my father." I'd been thinking the words and they spilled out.

"Maybe that's something to think about doing. A funeral is a closing, offering comfort to a family. We celebrate the life of the departed, but a family needs to say good-bye."

"We never said good-bye," I said. "One day my father was there; the next, he was gone. Sometimes I feel like he never existed except in my imagination."

"Find some good memories, Elvira. Hold on to those. That will help to ease that burden you carry. I'm going to walk over and see to the girl's mother now. Think you can handle the rest of the peeling?"

I nodded. "Can I ask you something? Did Jessie help anyone today, see anything?"

"No," he answered. His voice was low, sad. "It's mysterious how these things work, Elvira. I know Connie's disappointed but I don't think seeing is something anyone can control. Like I said before, I think God gives Jessie the words when the words need saying. She can't make it happen and she doesn't see everything that's coming."

Maybe she didn't see everything that was coming but I knew what she'd done today. Jessie had clammed up, like back home when she didn't talk. She'd probably seen lots of things for those people in the tent. Maybe horrible things like starvation and war and little girls cracking their heads on rocks. But she kept it to herself instead of telling this time. She'd spoiled my mother's plan on purpose. I wished I had that kind of bravery to stand up to my mother like Jessie did. Maybe it was just like the preacher said and God gave the words when they needed saying, but Jessie had figured out how to stay silent if she wanted to. I didn't understand it. And I didn't understand God much, either. But there were times I wanted to like him just to have someone to talk to.

"I'm glad it didn't work, my mother's idea. I don't want Jessie to see sadness all the time." I thought again about the German lady's words.

"I know." He stood up to go, brushing potato peel off his pants. "I'm sure there'll be times when it's something happy, something good to look forward to. Think about that. God takes away, but God gives too."

I thought about that. I thought about God giving, and I wondered if he only gave to good people, people who prayed and read the Bible and never told lies.

I watched the preacher walk down the path. Maybe I'd been wrong about him. He wasn't so bad. I watched until I couldn't see him anymore and then I listened to the sounds of the approaching night. Birds twittered and the first crickets were coming out to sing. Someone laughed. Children shrieked in play. The wind whistled through the pines, and I heard the sharp snap of a burning log and smelled a hundred campfires.

For the first time in a long time, I felt safe.

Chapter 17

We got up early. A light rain had washed everything clean and the sun was warm, promising summer. In the distance, a meadowlark trilled, greeting the morning with song. Jessie helped me pick a bouquet of lady slippers, wood violets, and wild geraniums. The geranium petals were the pink of sunset. We plucked three wood violets and pressed them between the pages of the *Lutheran Ladies' Guild Cookbook* in memory of the little girl. I put the delicate purple flowers in the fancy desserts section, on the page with chocolate éclairs. It was a page I'd look at often.

We tied a length of white ribbon from Grandma's sewing basket around the bouquet, handed it to the preacher, and he placed it on the casket. The preacher wore the white suit he'd worn that first day at our house in Portage. It seemed so long ago. He stood on the fairgrounds stage behind a podium, shuffling papers, and waited for the crowd to be seated. His expression was calm, as if he'd done all his thinking and praying earlier and now had all the time in the world for this one service.

I'd never been to a funeral. I figured the funeral was a lot like church would be. People had tried to dress up, but it's hard to dress up when you're camping and there's nowhere to wash clothes except one bathroom sink. Most of the ladies wore hats, and those did look nice, bright colors against blue sky with netting veils casting shadows in little squares on their faces.

The girl's mother was sitting on a bench upstage from the preacher. Must be no father. Maybe that woman lost her husband in the war like my mother did. Now she'd lost her daughter too. I felt so sad for her. I knew what it felt like to lose someone. It hurt. Terribly.

The pine coffin, delivered by a St. Paul undertaker, was small and plain and nailed shut. It sat behind the preacher on two tables pushed together, high enough for everyone to see. It was hard to believe that little girl was in it.

I knew the girl's name now since I'd read the preacher's sermon. I knew why he'd wanted me to read it. It wasn't only for the little girl and her mother. There were things in that sermon for me.

A group dressed in white climbed the steps and filed onto the stage. Before I had a chance to wonder what they were doing, they started to sing "Amazing Grace," the prettiest song, in perfect harmony, deep voices and high voices blending together smooth as silk.

Jessie squirmed and I put my arm around her. I wanted to keep her close.

"You'll have to sit still, Jessie," I whispered, and she

snuggled closer. "A funeral is how everyone says good-bye. We have to be quiet out of respect."

"I already said good-bye," she whispered back, swinging her legs. I put my hand on her knee.

"You did? Okay, but we still need to let everyone else do the same thing." Jessie nodded, curls bouncing, her expression serious.

People wouldn't meet our eyes. They probably thought Jessie was a fake. Must be confusing since we traveled with the preacher. Preachers didn't lie. Did they?

My mother hadn't come to the funeral; she'd feigned a headache. I figured she was humiliated, since Jessie didn't go along with her plan. Once Jessie clammed up, there was no changing her mind. Now that everything had backfired I supposed my mother wished she'd never thought of the idea, charging for Jessie's seeing powers. "Wish in one hand, spit in the other, see which one gets filled first," Grandma always said.

I wondered how we'd get to California without any money. I still didn't know why we were going there, but it didn't seem to matter anymore. I'd go where Jessie went.

The preacher had placed a hat for an offering at the foot of the stage. He told the crowd whatever was collected would go to the dead girl's mother to help with future expenses. It seemed a much better cause to me than anyone paying for Jessie's seeing capabilities. I'd looked in the hat before we found our seats and there was loose change and a few dollar bills. Even Grandma put in a quarter.

Grandma sat on the other side of Jessie, still as stone. She didn't have a hat, but she wore a straight blue skirt and matching jacket with a white blouse. I'd never seen her dressed up. She'd coiled her hair and pinned a white hand-kerchief to cover her head. *A white handkerchief means truth.* The German lady's words stuck in my mind. I could tell Grandma didn't want to be there, but she'd come any-way, out of respect for the dead. She sat straight with her head held high, and she'd ignored the looks and whispers when we first sat down. I felt proud of her for that.

We stood for the Lord's Prayer. I didn't know the words but I pretended I did. Out of the corner of my eye I saw Jessie copying me, folding her hands, bowing her head. Sometime, I'd tell her what the preacher said about imag-ining God's home as a star in the sky. Praying to him there. Maybe I'd try it, see how it felt.

The preacher cleared his throat. "Today, we are here to celebrate life," he said. I recognized the opening lines of the sermon I'd read. "Today we celebrate the life of little Emma Neilson, taken from us when we least expected it, taken by God for reasons we can't comprehend. Taken from us but delivered to a better place, a place of peace and beauty and love. Ours is not to question why. Instead, our earthly duty is to keep her in our hearts and to trust in God that his need for her was greater than ours, his place more impor-tant than we can ever know. Until we, too, join him there."

People dabbed at their eyes. Folding chairs squeaked and a man coughed. A baby started to cry and I saw the mother clutch it close, rub its back to calm the fussing. It occurred to me that these were not bad people. We were all here for the same reason, a funeral, and none of us had asked for this. The preacher was letting us know that Emma Neilson's death was nobody's fault. I squeezed Jessie's shoulder.

"In life, Emma gave joy to her mother and her departed

father and those whose lives she touched. With God, joy is hers. With God, there is everlasting joy. This we must believe. This we must understand. For this is what keeps us plodding forward through wars and times of trouble and even death. This is faith. Please stand."

We stood. The preacher was so powerful; his voice boomed. I admired him. I believed in him. I wanted every-one to believe in him. He was telling all of us there's hope. Hope no matter what happens, no matter what life is like or when death comes. And he was telling us to keep the dead in our hearts.

I took Jessie's hand while we sang "Rock of Ages."

Suddenly, I remembered my father singing that hymn. I remembered the tune and the words.

I remembered him.

I sang loud. For my father.

He waved. My father waved from the edge, but he didn't try to save me. I gasped for air. Slipped deeper and deeper into cold, black water, my nose and ears and mouth filling, choking me, drowning me. I tasted salt. The panic and the fear dared me to sink into blackness. Give up. Close my eyes. But I kicked my feet and flailed, trying to swim to the surface, trying to reach the blinding flash of orange light I saw above. My hand touched something soft and giving. Something alive. I tried to scream but the water was heavy, smothering. My arms were lead, so tired, so tired. And my father waved from the shore. Not even trying to save me.

My eyes flew open. I could hardly breathe. My heart pounded so hard I thought surely it wouldn't keep beating.

Surely it would break, thumping like that. The dream was so real. My nightgown was twisted around my legs, sticking to me, damp with sweat. I sat up. Put my hand on my heart to calm the pounding. I breathed through my mouth until my skin tingled and I felt lightheaded.

There was enough moonlight in the tent to make out the sleeping forms of my mother and Jessie next to me. Grandma slept as far away from all of us as she could get, against the far tent wall and covered by blankets. She'd lined up a row of boxes between her spot and us, either for a tiny bit of privacy or as a fence to keep us out. I wasn't sure which. I saw the faint outline of her notebook. Her ballpoint was stuck in the spiral binding. She'd placed it close to her pillow as though she might need it in the middle of the night.

How could they sleep through my dream? In my head it was so loud — the rushing sound of the water, the splash of kicking to reach the surface. I went over each detail, each scene in my mind. There was a new part, something I'd never seen before. All the nights I'd had it, the dream was the same. Me drowning. My father above, waving. But that night in the dream my hand had touched something that moved. Something alive.

I was wide awake. Why didn't my father save me? I knew it was only a dream but I still wanted to know. It made me angry he didn't save me.

I glanced again at Grandma. She was snoring.

I crept over to my box of clothes, and as quietly as I could, I dug to the bottom. Pulled out my father's old brown parka. It was wrinkled and musty smelling. I buried my nose in it, searching for his scent, the one I remembered so well. There was nothing. No clean smell of bleached white undershirts, no Beech-Nut wintergreen mints, no whiskey. I felt the weight of my treasures in one pocket. I kept the German lady's white hanky in the other pocket. I checked to make sure everything was still there and the fabric rustled in my hands. My stomach flipped as my mother moaned and turned over. But she didn't wake up. I slipped my arms through the sleeves.

Grandma and my mother hadn't passed any notes today, but they still weren't speaking to each other. Why? Slowly, I reached over the boxes. Slid Grandma's notebook out from under her nose.

I had the feeling there was something in it I should know.

Chapter 18

I'd stolen Grandma's notebook, but I was afraid to read it. I did and didn't want to know what it said. The silence in the campground was eerie—the whoosh of the wind the only sound, and the moon shining through the pines in pale patches the only light. The air smelled faintly of skunk. It wasn't very cold but a shiver shook my body. Grandma told me an old superstition once: a shiver meant that someone was walking over your future grave site.

I drew my father's parka close, hunching down in the back of the preacher's truck so the side panels would hide me. The last thing I needed was to get caught spying. My fingers seemed to turn to the first page by themselves. I took a deep breath.

It was a note to my mother.

This is the dumbest thing you've ever done, Constance, Grandma had started off, and right away I could hear the sound of her voice as if she were criticizing my mother at that very moment. Like she always did. I couldn't think of one time in my entire life I'd heard her say something nice to my mother. What did she hate about her? Was it all because she married my father?

Grandma's handwriting was small and precise, slanted, with loops and curlicues reaching up or dropping down exactly halfway between each blue line on the notepaper. Like they taught in school. If she were in school, all the kids would hate her for that perfect penmanship. It was another reason they all hated me. Grandma's handwriting was just like mine.

My heart skipped and hairs on the back of my neck prickled. I shifted so moonlight lit the page.

A four-year-old child tells you to go see Ray, and you're ready to traipse across the country? He's dead, Constance. Get it through that thick skull. He's not coming back. He's not missing in action. I don't care what that telegram said. Ray is dead. Blown up. His bones are floating around the Pacific Ocean because sharks gobbled up his body five minutes after he hit the water.

It's been almost five years, for God's sake. How could you be so naïve as to believe he's alive just because Jessie says "go see Ray"? Face the facts. You're chasing a ghost. Don't you think the War Department would have found evidence if he were alive? This seeing thing has gotten out of hand. It's hogwash. I raised a fool. I went along with this because I thought it might do you good to leave Portage. Not because I

*believed you'd find Ray. God forbid. All you'd find
would be empty whiskey bottles. Either you give up
this ridiculous idea, or I'm leaving you and going back
to Portage. Unlike you, I do not believe in Jessie's pre-
dictions. What that child needs is a good spanking.
Someone has to think with a clear head. Too bad it's
always me.*

Bile rose in my throat. The words on the page blurred.
I was breathing fast and sweating in the parka. I started to
shake and took slow, deep breaths to calm myself down.
This could not be true. I wiped my eyes, squinted in the
low light, and read Grandma's note again.

My father was alive? How could that be?

My mother believed it. Jessie must've seen him in a
vision alive and well and waiting for us. Jessie must believe
it. Everything Jessie'd said so far had come true. Grandma
must be wrong and Jessie right. We were going to California to find my father. And Grandma had to go, just like
Jessie'd said. To see. Grandma had to go with us to see my
father alive.

The metal panel of the preacher's truck was digging
into my spine. I adjusted my position and as I did, a brown
piece of paper fell from Grandma's notebook. It was the
scrap of paper sack I'd handed to my mother when the line
of people waited to see Jessie. It was my mother's answering note. I smoothed the wrinkles.

*Oh, isn't this just so typical of you. Keep your real
feelings hidden until it's too late to change anything.
You should never have come in the first place then.
I should never have expected you to believe what I*

know to be true. Jessie saw Ray, Mom. She heard the
song. I'm the only one who ever heard it before. He
wrote it for me on the day we got married. She could
never have known about it. She saw him.

He's there. I know he is. I don't care if you believe
it. I don't care if you stay or not. But Elvira and Jessie
do. Can you abandon them? Like my father aban-
doned you? You're a bitter old woman. Why don't you
think of someone else beside yourself for a change?
Oh, I can hear you saying, "There's the pot calling the
kettle black," but if I'm selfish, I learned it from you.
I'm sick of these notes. I'm tired of your criticizing. I
will find Ray and we will be a family again. With or
without you.

— Connie

My mother's pencil point had broken on the word *self-*
ish. I remembered the look on her face. How she'd had to
keep her anger inside with all those people watching. I read
Grandma's letter one more time. Her words were mean
and hurtful, and I was sick and tired of the way she treated
my mother. I didn't need her. My mother was wrong about
that. I wouldn't miss Grandma one bit if she abandoned us.
Bitter old woman.

Suddenly I felt light, happy, as if I would float on the
slightest breeze.

For the first time in a long time, I was on my mother's
side.

But what if she was wrong? No. She wasn't wrong. He
must be alive.

First thing, I'd tell my father how sorry I was for making

him leave. *I didn't mean for you to run away,* I'd say. *I was just talking without thinking back then when I was little. I'm older now. I would never say that now. I should have stopped you that morning. Please forgive me.* I'd say all that and he'd answer, *Aw, now, Elvira, no use crying over spilled milk.* Then he'd hold my hand. We'd walk, talking and catching up. He'd tell me where he'd been all this time. We'd sing "Blueberry Hill," look at my treasures, and bring back all the good memories we shared.

I was going to get another chance. God *must* be real. He was giving my father back to me.

I was going to be forgiven.

My father was alive.

He was. I believed it. Didn't I?

Chapter 19

Y ou're chipper this morning," said the preacher. He'd just come back from washing and had one of our towels draped around his shoulders like he was part of the family.

It was early, but the morning seemed brighter, sunnier than most days. The pines looked greener, and clouds, white like just-bleached pillowcases, swept across a bluer-than-blue sky. Was I just noticing these things or did happiness make everything prettier?

"I got a good sleep," I said.

I didn't like to lie to the preacher. The truth was I hadn't slept much at all. After reading the notes, I'd spent the rest of the night thinking about seeing my father again. I pictured him clean-shaven with his hair slicked back. Sitting on the porch of a yellow house. The house I'd always imagined. He was waiting for me. In my mind, I saw him run a hand through his hair to catch a stray strand and then leap up to meet me as I opened the gate in the white picket fence. I could feel his hug. Smell his just-washed clothes.

I pictured him kissing my mother's cheek. She'd look up at him in an adoring way, all swoony like a movie star, with her arm around his waist, and say she loved him better now that he'd sworn off whiskey forever. I saw Grandma, eating crow and apologizing for doubting us.

What would my father think of Jessie, having not met her before? He'd recognize his own green eyes in hers. Would he swoop her up in a hug as well?

I shook off the nagging feeling that my sister's vision couldn't be true. I'd spent half the night weighing the possibilities: he'd gotten amnesia and didn't know who he was for all that time; he'd been lost in California and had no way to get home; maybe he was blind and couldn't write letters; or maybe they had him mixed up with somebody else all this time and they just found out he had a family. Everything I came up with sounded far-fetched. But Jessie must be right. There was no other answer — he must be alive. I wanted to believe it. And the German lady had said listen to Jessie. Surely she meant this.

"Elvira? You dreaming?"

I smiled at the preacher. I liked him. I would have liked anybody at that moment. But I wasn't about to tell him my father was alive. The preacher was kind but he wasn't family, with or without our towel around his shoulders. When we got to California we'd say thank you very much for the ride, and he could get on his way.

"When are we leaving?" I asked.

Jessie skipped out of the tent kicking up clouds of dust,

hair all mussed, singing a little ditty in her high voice. Mabel dangled from her hand. In her other hand she carried the whistle the preacher had carved for her. He'd been teaching her to play snappy tunes. There weren't many notes on the whistle but she could play "Twinkle, Twinkle, Little Star" and "Row, Row, Row Your Boat." She'd picked those tunes up quickly. Jessie was musical, like my father. The two of them were going to like each other.

"We're going today. We're going today. We're going out California way."

Jessie found a patch of sunlight and danced around in a circle, laughing and spinning and waving her arms like she used to back home. The German lady said children should laugh and play and go to school. Not see sadness all the time. Jessie dancing reminded me I was the big sister and maybe it was up to me to make her life fun. Maybe it was up to me to have some fun myself. But I had a delicious secret. I wasn't going to tell anyone that I knew my father was alive. That would be fun enough for a while. I didn't even care that Jessie hadn't told me what she knew. Nothing mattered except seeing my father again.

I grabbed Jessie's hand and twirled her around. Picked her up and danced her through the campsite. The preacher pounded a beat on the picnic table and sang "In the Mood." "Da, da, da, da, da, da, in the mood." It was the perfect song for that moment, full of hope and the promise of good things to come.

The two barefoot boys from next door were watching from the shadows. They had solemn expressions like they'd never had any fun their entire lives. I'd barely glanced at them when Jessie stiffened in my arms. She went rigid and her knees jabbed me in the ribs. I put her down gently, as if she might break.

Jessie walked over to the boys. They didn't say a word. Only stared at her. She stared right back. That same glassy-eyed look I'd seen before.

"You can go home," she said to them. "It will be all right now. Nobody's taking the farm. Your daddy can save it. Tell him to put in feed corn. You go home and put in feed corn. The money will come from that."

The boys turned and ran.

I looked at the preacher. I remembered what he'd said about Jessie seeing good things too sometimes, and that God gives Jessie the words when the words needed saying. He nodded, as if to say, *See?*

I took Jessie's hand, and we skipped all the way to the bathroom for a wash.

We met my mother coming out. Her face was scrubbed. She wore red lipstick and a clean dress; the pale blue color suited her. I wanted my mother to know I was on her side, not Grandma's. Like her, I wanted to believe my father was alive. I'd never doubt Jessie, either. But I couldn't tell my mother I'd stolen the notes. She'd be furious.

"Don't take long, you two," she said. "We've got to go to town for supplies before we leave, and we have a long drive today. I want to get as far as possible before dark."

I wanted to speed up the leaving too. "Maybe I can get supplies with the preacher while you and Grandma and Jessie pack up," I said. "If you give us a list, we can make it fast."

"Well, that's helpful, Elvira. What's gotten into you?"

I shrugged. She didn't know I was on her side. It didn't

matter. I'd rather go for supplies with the preacher than be around Grandma anyway.

℘

Sitting in the cab of the truck was much better than riding in the back with the wind and the dust. Bumpy, though. Every time the preacher shifted gears, the truck jerked, and his empty cooler slid from side to side in the back. I held the armrest to keep from bouncing off the seat. Good thing we didn't have far to go. The truck rattled to a stop in front of a general store right next to a tavern. The tavern had double doors with iron handles but no windows. "Paulson's Tavern" in orange neon cast a strange glow on the bricks of the building even though it was daylight. A wooden sign said "Bets, Billard, and Cards" in hand-painted letters.

"What's a billard?" I asked.

The preacher chuckled. "I think the proprietor meant billiards. Like pool. Ever seen a pool table? No? It's sort of a parlor game. In both pool and billiards, you use a cue stick, but in billiards, you hit three balls across a felt-covered table and drop them into pockets on the side. In pool, there are eight balls. You rack them up differently. Not a bad game but the establishments where you find billiards can be shady."

"You mean like bars?"

"Yes, like bars. Got the list?"

How did the preacher know about a game played in shady places? As he held the door, I looked around the neighborhood. A pawnshop with dirty windows was across the street. It was closed. Maybe everyone around here already pawned all they owned. I saw a sweet shop that looked clean and inviting. The street was gloomy, though, and mostly deserted.

"Sort of a seedy part of town, isn't it?" said the preacher. "We'll get the things on Connie's list and be on our way."

He took my elbow to guide me through the door of the store as if I couldn't walk on my own. Like he was protecting me.

We bought flour, milk, bacon, a flat of eggs, and apples. Two loaves of white bread and a pound of butter. Campbell's canned soup for twelve cents a can: tomato, ham with broccoli — which I hated — and split pea soup — which I could tolerate if it was all we had. I read from the list while the preacher pulled items from the shelves and placed them neatly in our cart. Sharp cheddar cheese, navy beans, a can of Maxwell House Coffee, and sugar. A sign tacked to the shelf said the sugar ration was lifted. It was still expensive but the preacher didn't flinch as he grabbed a five-pound bag. Jugs of maple syrup sat on the shelf next to the sugar. My mouth watered for buttermilk pancakes. It had been ages since I'd made them and even though I knew the recipe by heart, it would be comforting to pull out the *Lutheran Ladies' Guild Cookbook*.

"Do you like buttermilk pancakes?"

"You bet. Why?"

"If we buy a quart of buttermilk and some baking soda, I can make pancakes for breakfast tomorrow." I tried not to look too hopeful.

"We'd need maple syrup then," he said, taking a jug off the shelf, grinning as he added it to the cart. I grabbed a box of Arm 'n' Hammer Baking Soda before he could

change his mind and wheeled the cart down the aisle, back
to the dairy section, where I plucked a quart of buttermilk.

"Be right back," said the preacher, disappearing around
a corner. I groaned when he returned with a big sack of
potatoes.

"How are we going to practice our peeling techniques if
we don't buy potatoes?" he asked.

"We could peel apples? Bet it's easier."

"Spoil sport."

I realized I was having fun. My spirits had soared since
I found out my father was alive. I couldn't wait to see him.
What if when we found him he still drank whiskey? No. I
wouldn't think about that. We bought a block of ice for the
cooler and paid, the preacher pulling a twenty-dollar bill
out of his wallet. He only got a few pennies back in change.
I held the door for him this time. The clerk had packed a
huge box, and it made the cart too heavy for me to push.

A man flew out of Paulson's Tavern and landed on the
sidewalk. Another man, raging mad, burst through the
double doors, kicked the man in the stomach, and wiped
his hands on a dirty apron stretched across his huge belly.
"You're cut off, pal. Don't be coming around here again.
Whiskey ain't free and nobody insults Pauly." He didn't
even glance at us as he stalked back inside.

The man had a bloody nose. The preacher dumped
the box of groceries in the back of the truck and tried to
help him up. The man shook the preacher off, staggered
to his feet, and walked unsteadily down the sidewalk. He
stopped to lean on the wall of the tavern, bent in half, then
rushed to the gutter and vomited. I turned my head. It was
disgusting. I knew why he was sick.

"I'm sorry you had to see that," said the preacher.

"I've seen it before." It slipped out. I felt like I'd betrayed my father.

"Yes, I suppose you have."

How did he know? I felt a knot in my stomach. My mother had been telling stories. Did she tell the preacher any good things about my father? I could tell him plenty and when we found him, he wouldn't be drinking.

"How about we chance that sweet shop and get a chocolate malt? We still have time before we need to be back."

My mother would be mad if we dawdled but I didn't feel like going back yet either. I nodded. A chocolate malt was worth the risk of my mother's anger.

The sweet shop had a candy counter up front and a full soda fountain with swivel stools, but the preacher chose a red vinyl booth near the back. We sipped our malts, the creamy chocolate a treat to my tongue. The malts were so thick, the waitress had given us long spoons as well as straws. We each had a metal shaker that held the extra. I loved the idea there'd be more when the glass was empty.

"Want to taste mine?" said the preacher.

"We have the same thing," I said, rolling my eyes.

"Right." He twirled his straw. Stirred his malt with the spoon. "My father was a drinker too. I know what it's like to grow up in a house like that," he said, dabbing at the edges of his mouth with a paper napkin. He stared straight at me with an intense, serious look in his eyes, so different than his jovial mood of the past hour. "You never know what's going to happen and everything always feels like it's your fault. Even small things. Unimportant things like if you accidentally break your father's pipe when you're

147

cleaning it, and it throws him into a drunken fit of rage, and he beats you with the belt he's got handy."

"Did that happen to you?" I couldn't imagine a father so horrible.

"Yes. That and more. But it was drink that fueled his rage. There was good in him too. Other times. Dry times."

I nodded. I understood that.

"He was a minister. Had a large congregation. People believed in him. Followers didn't know he was different at home."

I'd never talked to anyone like this. Why was the preacher telling me? "Where was your mother?"

"Left when I was two. I never knew her. He raised me himself. He did the best he could, I suppose. As I got older, we didn't see eye to eye on anything." The preacher shifted in the booth. Put his elbows on the table and curled his hands around his glass. "Above all, we disagreed about God. His was a fiery and furious God. A punishing God. I believed differently. Still do. Even though sometimes I have to shake up a gathering with the word *damnation*, I serve a gentle, nurturing God. One who would hold your hand and whisper."

"Like a friend?"

"Yes. Like a friend. There's only one God. But people see God the way they want to."

"Is that why you decided to be a traveling preacher? So you could be different than your father?" I understood that too. I didn't want to be like my mother.

He chuckled, crinkles showing at the corner of his eyes. "That's probably one reason. But I always felt it was a calling. Something I needed to do. You know what I wish?"

I didn't know preachers made wishes. "What?"

"Someday I'd like to have a church of my own. Just a little church. Pretty, with a steeple and maybe a stained glass window or two. Enough well-crafted, comfortable pews. Congregation that gathers every Sunday to visit with friends and because they enjoy being in a house of God. I'd like that."

The way he described it, I'd like to see a church like that. I slurped the last of my malt through the straw, making a loud sucking sound. I wasn't embarrassed. The preacher made the same sound with his straw. He reached across the table and put his hand on mine.

"When I was traveling in Virginia in '42, I met a fellow doing fine work with folks who drink too much. Name was Bob. Never got his last name. He was a doctor and he had a partner along with him. The two of them started a fellowship called Alcoholics Anonymous. AA for short. Their methods seemed to help folks."

The preacher removed his hand and picked up his napkin. Tore off tiny bits and made a pile like jagged snowflakes on the gray Formica tabletop.

"First a person has to admit they're powerless over drink. Bob said someone will only stop drinking if they want to and they admit that first step. No one else can change them. Not a wife. Not a child. Since I heard that, I've felt better. I always thought I should've been able to stop my father's drinking, but Bob said children always think the drinking is their fault. He said entire families live in denial, and denial is the strangest state of mind. People believe what they want to believe to make it all okay, disregarding facts even if the facts are staring them in the face.

An alcoholic lives in denial too, believing they can stop drinking anytime. But denial creates false hope. Might be too late for your father and mine, but with AA there's real hope for some, at least."

"I'm glad," I said. I'd always thought I could change my father too. It wasn't my fault he drank whiskey. I felt that old guilt lifting. It settled back a second later. It *was* my fault he enlisted. But God was giving him back to me. Mrs. Keller had asked God to watch over me. Did this mean he was? Would I have to pay God back by being good forever? I might never forgive myself for making my father leave, but at least I'd have a chance to say I was sorry. Maybe God would notice that.

We stood up. The preacher swept the bits of napkin into his palm and dumped them in the empty metal shaker. "Someday, when I get that little church, maybe I'll set up a meeting room for people who need the kind of help AA offers. Seems like something God might approve of."

It did sound like something God would approve of.

Suddenly, it hit me that I'd started to believe in God. When had that happened? Some of it still didn't make sense. But it didn't matter. Believing felt good.

I liked the preacher's God.

I'd keep his God for my own.

Chapter 20

My mother said thank you to the preacher when we returned with supplies, placing her fingertips on his arm and smiling, but she glared at me. We took too long. She was in a hurry to get on the road. Even facing her anger now, I was glad I'd gone with the preacher and heard his story. I'd find a way to thank him before he left us.

I'd never really thought about other people having fathers who drank. I'd try to stop blaming myself for my father's drinking, but the memories of tiptoeing and bringing him coffee and wishing he'd stay still lingered in my mind. I knew the preacher was telling the truth. I couldn't have changed my father. It did feel better hearing that, but it might take me a while to believe it.

Another reason I was glad I went with the preacher was that the tents were down, boxes packed, and it didn't take long to load the truck.

"C'mon, Jessie," I said. "Help me make a fort with the boxes to block the wind."

She climbed into the back. Helped shove the preacher's cooler to the tailgate and drag boxes into a square with a seating area for us in the middle. I made a bed for Mabel on a pillow. Tucked the corners under a box so the pillow wouldn't fly out. I still hadn't made Mabel a dress. "I promise when we stop for the night, we'll get started on clothes for Mabel, okay?"

"Okay. Grandma has scraps."

"I know. Maybe we'll cut up an old blouse instead. We'll see." I was avoiding Grandma. We didn't need her scraps. We might need her scissors, though. I hadn't thought of that.

A few people came to shake the preacher's hand. Nobody said good-bye to us. The family next door was gone. I hoped Jessie was right about the boys' father saving the farm. Of course she was right. She always was. Wasn't she? We settled into our spots as the preacher's truck clanked and bumped through the gates of the St. Paul fairgrounds and headed west.

We weren't ten miles out of Minneapolis when the sky rumbled and turned instantly black, spitting icy raindrops from nowhere, stinging our faces and sending Jessie and me scrambling for our blankets in the back of the truck. We covered our heads and huddled, our backs up against the cab, and watched lightning split clouds, turning the highway and fences and fields a ghostly blue. Jessie jumped with every crash of thunder. Her eyes were fearful. She was shaking when she grabbed my hand and held tight. Our blankets were soaked in minutes, and we felt the truck sway as the preacher braked on water that ran in sheets across the road.

That's when we saw the dog.

Jessie screamed.

"Stop!" she yelled and screamed again.

No one heard her over the storm. The poor dog was frantic and dirty, running from the storm and the thunder, racing the truck right alongside the rear wheel. Saliva bubbled from the sides of its mouth. There was nothing we could do. The truck hit a slick and slid right into the dog, knocking it off its feet. I watched the dog skid in a heap to the edge of the road.

Jessie and I both screamed this time. I stood up and hammered on the cab window and banged on the top of the truck. Screamed so loud my throat hurt as the dog became a smaller and smaller dot behind us.

But the preacher heard.

He looked over his shoulder at Jessie and me standing up in the truck, holding on for dear life. Braked from the look on our faces. That look must've scared him half to death.

He backed up all the way to the dog. We got out and stood in the rain looking down at the body. It was a silent, mucky lump with a smashed head. Blood flowed from the wound and mixed with the rain and the mud. I felt so sorry we'd killed it. I swallowed tears and tasted salt. I knelt in the gravel by the side of the highway and whispered "Sorry" in the dog's ear and touched a silky eyelash and stroked the matted, yellow fur.

And the soaked tail thumped. Once.

Then the tail thumped again.

Weak, like it took a huge effort. I jumped up and said, "This dog is alive. Quick, get it in the truck."

For some reason, everyone listened to me. Even Grandma kept her wisecracks to herself.

We heaved that dog onto the old Hudson Bay blanket and carried it to the truck.

స్

We probably should've tried to find the owners. We probably should've waited out that storm and knocked on every farmhouse door in the county. But we didn't. Somebody cared well for that dog once because that dog smiled and wagged and slobbered Jessie and me with love. I felt a little guilty about that.

She took a particular liking to me.

I named her Sarah, the name I'd always wanted for myself. It was a foolish name, too formal for a mangy yellow lab. But I adored that name and I adored that dog. Sarah wasn't hurt as bad as we'd first thought. Since the preacher was the one who'd hit her, he felt responsible for her well-being. "Every kid needs a dog," he whispered to me like we shared that secret knowledge. I couldn't have agreed more. The preacher took over the dressing of the wound, fussing about keeping it clean and covered. Showed me how to make Sarah lie still while we drove. I pulled her heavy body on my lap and held her head between my knees, feeding her bits of leftover buttermilk pancakes, which she seemed to love.

The preacher talked my mother into keeping Sarah. "It's a good idea to have a dog along on a road trip," he said. "For protection." I knew he made that up but it worked. For once, my mother didn't protest. She listened to the preacher. He seemed to calm her nerves when she was riled.

Grandma made Jessie and me wash our hands more often, and she held her nose when Sarah was near to prove the point about unclean pets carrying diseases.

Sarah could've carried a plague for all I cared. It felt like I'd finally found a friend. The preacher stopped at a market and picked up a big bag of Gaines Dog Meal, apparently America's favorite dog food and more nutritious than pancakes. Sarah ate from my mother's cast-iron frying pan, which my mother only let Sarah use after I promised that a boiling water-and-vinegar mixture would kill any dog germs. I showed her the Household Tips section in the *Lutheran Ladies' Guild Cookbook* so she knew I wasn't making that up.

By the time we got to the Idaho border, Sarah was healed, demonstrating her renewed health by leaping and licking my face. She chased sticks every night when we stopped to camp by the side of the highway. She was gentle with Jessie, but she was wild with me. As though she knew she could get me to play, daring me to get in trouble, distracting me when I was supposed to be cooking or scrubbing pots or packing up so we could move on. Sarah helped with the boredom of the road and the waiting to see my father.

Should I thank God for giving Sarah to me or the preacher for hitting her? I was still confused about God's part in everything. But it didn't matter. I'd never felt so happy.

On the outskirts of Spokane, the preacher found a

community park that offered free camping. There were water spigots for filling coffeepots and washing dishes. No showers, but there were clean restrooms and a playground. Swings, a dented old merry-go-round, and a teeter-totter sat in sand, and there were picnic tables clustered under a canopy of elms.

I still hadn't made Mabel a dress. I'd been avoiding Grandma and was too preoccupied with Sarah. But we needed Grandma's sewing scissors, and I couldn't put off asking for them any longer.

"I promise after supper, we'll sit at one of those picnic tables and make that dress for Mabel. We can play on the teeter-totter too."

Jessie showed her seashell baby teeth. Sarah stood next to her, wagging her tail and whacking Jessie on the bottom with each wag. "Sarah," said Jessie, giggling. "Stop it." Sarah only wagged with more enthusiasm when Jessie said her name. We laughed and Jessie scampered off to help unpack for the night. Sarah looked at me, her wrinkled brow asking permission to follow.

That dog was smart. She sensed my moods. "Go on then," I said, shooing her.

Sarah raced after Jessie. So did I. It felt good to run. In my mind I heard my father's voice. "Race!" I'd put my doubts aside. My father would love Sarah.

Chapter 21

Dusk settled on the park while I was drying the supper dishes. It seemed to stay light longer the farther we drove west, and at this time of evening the sun turned everything golden. It would be wonderful to lean on the trunk of an elm and read *A Tree Grows in Brooklyn*. Pretend I was the main character, Francie Nolan, sitting on her balcony under her Tree of Heaven. What a glorious name for a tree. But I'd promised Jessie, and there was still about an hour to work on Mabel's dress before it would be too dark to see. That book would be out of print before I even had a chance to read past the third page, but somehow, stalling still gave me the feeling I could keep Mrs. Keller with me longer.

Sarah chased around, enjoying the expanse of grass, sniffing at the base of every tree, snapping at bugs. A group of children played a game of tag at the other end of the park, but Sarah wasn't bothering them, and they didn't seem curious about us. The park sat at the end of a pleasant street, neat houses with mowed lawns and swept porches. Maybe my yellow house would be on a street like this one. I couldn't wait to sit with my father on the porch of that house.

The preacher pushed Jessie on a swing. She squealed, "Higher!" He was teaching her to pump her legs, telling her to reach for the sky. It should've been me teaching her that, but it really didn't bother me it was the preacher instead. He was so kind to Jessie. And he stayed right behind as she pumped, working her legs into a rhythm, curls flying. If she fell, he'd catch her. I trusted the preacher with Jessie.

I dried the last dish and put it in the box.

"Tell your mother we're out of dish soap. She'll need to get some first thing. Won't even be able to do the breakfast dishes. Never plans ahead, that one."

I rolled my eyes. Grandma and my mother still weren't speaking. We were at the water spigot but my mother was five feet away, getting blankets out. Not that we'd need them tonight. The evening air was warm and dry. "I'll tell her." My mother glanced over. She'd already heard.

"May I borrow your sewing scissors? And a needle and thread? I promised I'd make Mabel a dress." The first words I'd said to Grandma in days.

She raised her eyebrows and pursed her lips. "I suppose. Those are the only scissors I have. Be careful not to break them. And don't snap a needle. They don't grow on trees, you know."

I wanted to remind her I was fourteen, not two. But I thanked her and unearthed her sewing basket from the truck. In Jessie's clothes box, I found a sleeveless blouse, white cotton with yellow daisies and pale-green leaves. Used to be mine and now it was even too small for Jessie. The collar was frayed and there was a tear in an underarm seam. My mother wouldn't say no to cutting up this blouse. Not that I was going to ask. I'd explain later if I had to. The fabric was perfect for a doll dress.

I spread the fabric on a picnic table and smoothed it with my hand. Threaded a needle. Cut a long rectangle and two shorter ones. I pictured the dress. It would be a sundress with a gathered skirt and a bodice, with a narrow waistband and shoulder straps. Snaps would hold the straps to the bodice so Jessie could undo them and pull the dress over Mabel's head. Maybe buttons on the straps for decoration, if Grandma would let me have some. In my mind, I saw Mabel wearing the finished dress. It seemed easy enough.

Jessie bounced over. "Are you making the dress? Wait, wait, Mabel wants to watch." Jessie propped Mabel against Grandma's sewing basket. "Can I help?"

"When it comes to the sewing, okay? Let me do the cutting." I cut two narrow strips for the shoulder straps. Put them aside, picked up the large rectangle, and held it up to Mabel. It was too long so I trimmed an inch off but left room for a hem. "We start with the skirt, see? I'll show you how to gather." There was a tiny stain on the fabric. I'd sew a pocket to cover it. I started stitching.

"Your stitches are too tight, Elvira. You'll never get that to gather if that's what you're trying to do. Thread will break."

"Are you going to help, Grandma?" said Jessie.

I could've smacked her. I didn't need Grandma's help. Sarah meandered over and settled at my feet. Sarah always seemed to know when I needed her.

"Fine. I'll loosen them up."

"You'll have to go back and take out those first stitches. Your gathers will bunch up if you don't. Are you sure you cut that piece long enough? Once it's gathered, it's shorter than you'd think. Haven't you ever sewn before?"

I felt like throwing the whole thing in Grandma's face. But Jessie said, "You teach Vira, Grandma. She already sees Mabel's dress in her mind. You help her make it."

"Oh? You can see it? Funny, that's how it always was with me. I could picture a dress and lickety-split, I'd have the finished piece. A perfect fit and it always looked exactly as I'd seen it in my mind. I made all your mother's clothes when she was young. They looked store-bought. Or like fancy Sears catalog clothes. Trims and notions are the key to a professional-looking garment. Your mother never appreciated that. And of course, your mother never showed any interest in sewing so I gave up trying to teach her."

Jessie hummed and made Mabel dance on the picnic table. I handed the fabric rectangle to Grandma. "Here, you make it then." But she surprised me.

"No, Elvira. You make it. Start by pulling out those stitches." I pulled them out, clipping carefully so as not to slice the skirt fabric. "May I just show you the stitch size? Two or three for an example and then you do the rest?" Grandma took the needle and thread but she didn't make a stitch until I nodded. Why was she acting nice?

Jessie smiled. Grandma didn't notice but I did. Had Jessie planned this?

It took me that night and the next to finish, but Mabel's dress was beautiful. The skirt was full, the hem even, and it fit perfectly. Grandma'd shown me how to turn the waistband and straps so the seams were neat. She'd also suggested criss-crossing the straps in back for a modern look. She was right about trims and notions too. I'd added yellow buttons to hide the stitching where the straps connected in front and a green ribbon bow on the pocket. I sewed rickrack in the same green shade as the bow along the bottom of the skirt. Even though Mabel was still filthy, the dress was perfect. Jessie was thrilled and she scampered off, swinging Mabel in her new dress. I felt proud. It turned out exactly as I'd pictured it.

I handed Grandma's sewing basket back. "Thanks," I said.

"You're welcome. I can turn you into a seamstress if you're interested," she said. "Seems you have a knack, like I always did. I even made your mother's wedding dress, you know."

I was interested. I knew Grandma once worked at the Portage Woolen Mills, but that was a long time ago and just factory work. Not professional sewing like making a wedding dress. The problem was, I didn't know how to admit I was interested in learning and still stay mad at her at the same time. "What did the wedding dress look like?"

Grandma picked at a loose piece of straw on the side of her sewing basket. Didn't look at me. "I have a picture, still. It was my masterpiece. Would have cost a fortune in a department store."

"May I see the picture?" If Grandma hated my father

161

so much, why did she make my mother's wedding dress? I wanted to ask her. But I wanted to see the picture more. Grandma turned away. I thought she was dismissing me, but she stepped to the preacher's truck, put the sewing basket on the tailgate, and beckoned to me. I sat down beside her. Glanced around to see where my mother and the preacher were.

Tonight, we were camped in a clearing by the side of the road. It had been hard to leave the comfort of the park, but at least there was a creek bubbling nearby where dragonflies flitted, translucent wings drumming the air. It was cool after the heat of the day, and a path, bordered by purple vetch that tumbled from blackberry thickets, wove through the shade of oaks.

The three of them were walking down the path, their backs to Grandma and me. Jessie skipped ahead and the preacher called something to her, but I couldn't hear what it was. It was getting dark. I didn't expect them to be gone long. Why was I feeling guilty for asking to see a picture of my mother's wedding dress? But Grandma must've felt the same way, because she drew the picture from the bottom of the basket and shielded it with her other hand.

I gasped and felt tears coming. My father was in the picture. He looked so young, fresh and clean like a boy ready for church. He wore a jacket and narrow tie and a wide smile. His arm was around my mother's shoulders. She leaned into him, and I could almost see her eyes sparkle.

"See, this was the hemline that was in fashion that year," Grandma said, pointing to the flare below the knee on the dress. "Very flattering. And the cap sleeves extended the shoulder. I used a sheer white organdy for those. 'Course,

Connie was skinny as a rail so the style accentuated her hips and waist. Looked good on her. I beaded the bodice with hundreds of silver glass beads. Mail order. Lined the entire dress with silk. Best work I ever did."

I tore my eyes away from my father. It *was* a beautiful dress. I'd never seen one like it. Not even in magazines. My mother looked like a movie star, elegant and happy. As though she didn't have a care in the world. "It's ... marvelous, Grandma. I don't know what else to say."

"Yes. It was a lovely dress. Long gone now. Just as well. A wedding dress brings back bad memories."

I looked at the picture again. It didn't look like a bad memory to me.

Jessie burst from the trees, skipping and playing a tune on her whistle. Mabel was sticking out of her shirt, orange hair flailing as Jessie hopped. The preacher and my mother were behind, shoulders almost touching as they walked, my mother's hair loose and wavy down her back. Grandma grunted. "Fool," she said, and mumbled something else I couldn't hear.

"What did you say?"

"Nothing," she answered. "Nobody listens to me anyway. I said nothing."

"Thank you for showing me the picture of the dress," I handed it back.

"Keep it. I don't need it anymore," Grandma said, and she walked off.

I stuffed the picture into my pocket. Later, I'd slip it into the pages of *A Tree Grows in Brooklyn*, right next to the paragraph about Francie's Tree of Heaven. I'd keep it forever.

Chapter 22

When we reached western Washington, the worst of the mountains were behind us. The preacher's truck had chugged to make every crest, overheating on the highest peaks. The engine churned and groaned, its radiator spewing white steam until we'd have to pull over and let the truck cool down. But once we hit the valleys the preacher picked up speed and the radiator seemed fine, only needing water from a jug every time we stopped for gasoline. By Seattle we were so dirty we smelled like goats, but we kept going, heading south toward California.

I couldn't stop staring at the picture of my mother and father. Scrunched down in the back of the truck with Sarah at my side, I showed it to Jessie, holding it tightly so it wouldn't fly from my hands and be lost forever.

"Mmmm, hmmm," she said. "Pretty dress."

"Don't you think Ray is handsome?"

Wind whipped Jessie's curls and it was hard to hear over the rattle of the truck. "Yes, handsome."

"Is that all you have to say about it?" She acted as if she'd seen the picture a million times. As if she'd seen my father a million times. I put the picture back in *A Tree Grows in Brooklyn* and closed the flaps on my box. I'd keep the picture for myself.

"Pretty dress," Jessie said again and clammed up.

We bumped along for two more days. My mother was anxious to get there and her nervousness spread like wildfire, settling on everyone else. It was as if we caught a jumpy disease, everyone except Jessie short-tempered and fed up. Startled by the smallest sounds. When Sarah barked at a fox running across the highway, I jumped clear out of my skin. I was sick of counting mailboxes and highway signs. Sick of playing alphabet games with Jessie in the back of that truck.

Oregon scenery was pretty — pine trees and jagged cliffs and rivers winding far below the highway, the damp, cool air smelling of moss — but the sameness wore on and on, and I kept drifting off to sleep. Grandma still wasn't speaking to my mother. An argument might liven things up but they ignored each other. Must've made it hard for the preacher, since he was the one stuck up front with them on that long and tedious drive.

Even Sarah was in a bad mood. She growled at Grandma every time we stopped for supplies or gasoline or to use a filling station restroom when one of us was about to burst. Sarah snarled like she blamed Grandma for the boredom. When Grandma wasn't looking, I petted Sarah for the effort. It felt good to blame someone. Wedding dress or not, I wasn't ready to forgive her. She was still a bitter old woman. Mean to my mother, mean to me. Most of the time, at least.

I tried to remember we were on our way to see my father and be a family again. I tried to keep that purpose in mind. Sometimes it seemed so fanciful. A little girl with seeing powers says to go see Ray and an entire family traipses across the country. I shook my fears off. Passed that kind of thinking to overtired boredom with grouchiness thrown on top. Imagined my father sitting on the porch of that pleasant yellow house I wanted instead.

I couldn't have been happier when we stopped in a tiny Oregon town to get gasoline and wash bugs off the windshield. My mother announced we'd be staying at a motel for the night. First one we saw.

"I need a bath," she said. "And something decent to eat. If I have to eat another potato, I think I'll scream."

It was true we'd had a lot of potatoes. Our suppers had been mostly beans and potatoes for days. I was craving something sweet like pie or ice cream, but treats were a distant memory. Would we ever sit down again to a real supper at a table with chairs? I was sick of sitting on the ground with rocks poking my bottom. I wanted real china plates. Fried chicken and green beans and maybe summer squash just for the color orange that looked so good with the green. And rhubarb pie for dessert. I could taste that imaginary dinner.

"How much longer until we get there?" I asked.

My mother looked at the preacher for an answer.

"Not much longer, Elvira," he said. "We'll cut over once we cross into California, right around Red Bluff, according to my map. There's a two-lane over to the coast. Connie wants to stop in Eureka. Pretty there, from what I hear. Dunes, lots of shells on the beaches. It's a fishing town."

Jessie started a chant. "Eureka, Eureka," she sang.

"Why Eureka?" I asked.

"Never mind, Elvira," my mother answered.

"Eureka, Eureka. Go see Ray," chanted Jessie.

My mother was horrified. Her cheeks turned the same color as the last chips of polish clinging to her nails. Floozy red. She turned her back to the filling station attendant. He was bustling around in clean, blue work pants and a freshly ironed blue shirt with "Al" stitched in red above the pocket. Al was wiping the oil stick with a rag. Although the hood of the preacher's truck was up, hiding his face, I knew Al was eavesdropping. We must've been a sight. One old woman, one younger woman, two girls, and a skinny preacher all in a beat-up truck piled high with debris. Everyone filthy and scrawny and bad-tempered.

"Go see Ray. Go see Ray."

"Stop, Jessie. Be quiet. Do not say that." My mother clamped her hand over Jessie's mouth. Her hand shook.

But it was too late. Jessie wiggled out of my mother's grasp.

Sarah barked. I rubbed her ears so she'd quiet down. She licked my hand.

"Go see Ray."

Grandma stomped to the truck, mumbling, "I guess that cat's out of the bag." She climbed in and slammed the door with a thunk. That was normal. It was the preacher I was worried about. He looked like he might be sick.

Jessie spun, kicking up gravel. "Eureka, Eureka. Go see Ray."

"What does she mean about Ray?" the preacher asked, moving close to my mother.

I'd never seen him angry. I'd never seen the vein in his forehead pop out and pulse as if a little river flowed there. I'd never seen nostrils flare like the preacher's did now. I imagined I could hear his heart thumping, but it was my own racing heartbeat in my ears. Would the preacher dump us and all of our boxes in the middle of that filling station? Al would tell us to take a hike. Maybe he'd call the sheriff and have us arrested for loitering.

The preacher would continue on by himself. He'd be furious at us for keeping him in the dark about our real reasons for hitching a ride.

He'd never forgive my mother. Or me.

"What does she mean, Connie?" he asked again, his voice shaky. Not at all like it usually was, deep and strong. Like when he read from the Bible or spoke his ideas and beliefs.

He put his hands in his pockets and looked my mother straight in the eye. She looked down at her feet. Wisps of hair escaped from her matted braid. She tucked them behind her ears impatiently. The preacher stepped closer, inches from her face, and put a hand on her arm. My mother looked up at him. I saw the flash of anger in her eyes, like a cornered animal. Her jaw was set. There was no changing her mind — I'd seen that look before.

"He's dead, Connie," the preacher said in a different voice, soft and soothing. The voice he used at the St. Paul revival when he spoke to the mother of the little girl. A voice for grief. "You can't believe Ray's still alive after all this time. You would have been notified. You're not being reasonable. It's false hope."

"Told you to listen to me, Connie." Grandma snuck back up and stuck her nose in like she'd always done back home. "Glad I'm not the only one who thinks this is a wild-goose chase. Pretty selfish act dragging us all the way across the country and not mentioning the real reasons she's been so nice to you, don't you think, Preacher? It's just like her to take advantage of a helping hand."

The preacher didn't answer Grandma. He didn't even acknowledge her presence.

I was scared. What if they were right? What if we'd come all this way and my father wasn't alive? But I was on my mother's side. Grandma didn't believe her. The preacher didn't believe her. She was only doing what Jessie said to do: go see Ray. Jessie'd been right about everything so far. I believed Jessie. I *had* to. Jessie was telling the truth. The German lady told me to listen to Jessie. I believed the German lady.

I believed my mother.

I moved between the preacher and my mother. Planted myself solid, folded my arms. Sarah sat down at my feet as though she was guarding me.

"If my mother says we're going to Eureka, we're going to Eureka," I said. "If my mother says my father is alive, then he is."

My mother put a hand on my shoulder. I felt warm and tingly from the weight of it there. It was so rare she touched me. I kept it like a prize, that good feeling. But the good feeling didn't last a minute.

"But what about us?" the preacher asked my mother. "What about our talks and plans? I thought ..."

"Don," my mother said. "I'm sorry."

It was the first time I'd heard the preacher's real name. It seemed strange for him to have one. He'd been nothing but "the preacher" for so long. Don. My mother'd called him Don. And it hit me. My heart lurched and I felt dizzy. I'd been so stupid. How could I have missed it?

The times they'd talked in low voices, stopping when I came near. How the preacher held my mother's elbow when she climbed into the truck and when they walked or sat together, their shoulders always touched. He'd called her a beautiful woman. Said I looked like her. He'd said my mother had a heart of gold. The way he stared at her with his eyebrows raised and a smile Grandma would call a Cheshire grin. He always stuck up for her when she was rude. Never questioned her decisions. Saw some good in her, something hidden to me.

The preacher was in love with my mother. He listened to her and laughed with her and brought her all this way. He was sweet on her. Maybe he wanted to marry her.

But we were going to my father. We were going to be a family again, going to live in a yellow house with a white picket fence and red roses in bloom. My father was never going to drink again. My mother was never going to yell or act mean or pour grease on my father's head. My father was alive. Waiting.

Waiting for me.

It didn't matter if the preacher loved my mother. She didn't care about his feelings. My mother was using the preacher to get her own way. She was selfish like Grandma said.

I wanted to tell the preacher, don't waste your time on her. She'll hurt you in the end. She only thinks of herself, take it from me. No heart of gold in that stone chest. But I couldn't tell him that. I had to stay on my mother's side.

It was the only way I'd ever get to my father.

Chapter 23

That night I had the dream. Maybe it was because I lay cramped on a canvas cot in a cheap motel room instead of sleeping on the hard ground like I was used to. It might've been the blue vacancy sign outside that kept me from getting solid rest. The sign flashed on and off, on and off, all night, lighting up the room through dirty beige drapes.

Maybe it was all the worry. Finding out the preacher loved my mother tied my stomach in knots. I felt bad for him. He'd been so kind to us. How could my mother let him fall in love with her? How could I betray him? What would God think of me now that I'd betrayed a preacher?

Maybe all the talk about my father stirred up the dream.

Whatever it was, I woke up sweaty and scared and angry. The motel room was ugly and smelled like mildew. The walls were painted a dead green and the flashing sign gave the room an eerie, underwater appearance. I gasped for air. The rushing sound in my ears was still loud like it was in the dream. I could see my father standing on the bank in orange light, waving like always. Ignoring me. He would not save me. I was drowning and he would *not* save me. I felt anger left over from the dream as my heart settled and my breathing slowed.

I had no right to be angry. But my father had every right to be angry with me for making him run away. Gone all these years. Alone. Was God punishing me for never telling my mother the truth about that day? Maybe that's why my father never saved me in the dream.

Again, my hand had touched something soft. Something living. I tried to remember, tried to see it as I sat there on the cot in that blue light, clutching my pillow to my chest. I closed my eyes. Pictured it. Struggling through water, arms flailing, legs kicking, trying to get to the bank where my father stood waving in the powerful orange light. Heavy water sucked me down, lower and lower where it was cold and frightening. And my hand touched something soft and dark. Something tangled. I couldn't get more than that. As hard as I tried, I could not remember anything else. I hated it.

I hated everything right then. My stomach hurt and a there was a persistent twang of pain in my lower back.

My mother slept with Jessie in one of the double beds. Grandma snored in the other. The preacher slept outside in the back of the truck with Sarah since pets weren't allowed in motel rooms. I felt guilty he'd agreed to taking care of Sarah after the way we'd treated him.

Not that Sarah could've done much damage to that

room. The bedspreads were worn beige chenille, the ribbed patterns down to bare fabric in places. Someone had taped a rip in the leather seat of an old wooden chair. The chair was missing a caster, making it tilt. I couldn't wait to leave. Get back on the road, find my father, and get on with our lives even if it meant we'd never see the preacher again.

The preacher didn't seem angry anymore. He hadn't left us behind and he was polite to my mother. He had more patience with her than I'd ever had. We'd kept going, through the last long, winding stretch of Oregon mountains, the preacher coasting and braking, coasting and braking, and after that truck had hauled us all across the country, chugging up rise after rise, it seemed unreasonable that the radiator boiled over on the final straightaway of US 99 before the California border. But it did.

We pulled over, everyone tumbled out, and the preacher got the water jug from behind his seat. He lifted the hood, steam billowing, water boiling over from the radiator cap, bubbling and spitting, dribbling through the engine onto the dirt shoulder of the road. He yanked his sleeve down over his hand, but it wasn't thick enough fabric to prevent the burn he got when he unscrewed the cap.

"Yow!" he'd yelled, flapping his hand, and I saw the blister forming. Jessie echoed his cry and Sarah barked in sympathy, but my mother and Grandma stood there, useless.

I ran to my box, pulled out *The Lutheran Ladies' Guild Cookbook*, and turned to the Household Tips section for the proportions. Mixed baking soda with water in a bowl and stirred it to a paste. Applied the paste where it was red and blistering and wrapped his hand in a strip of clean pillowcase. "There," I said. "Keep it covered." It was the least I could do after the way my mother had duped him.

"You're a good nurse," said the preacher, wincing, but smiling through the pain.

"You're kind of accident prone," I said, and immediately worried I'd offended him. But he laughed long and loud, his eyes crinkling at the corners, his old bruises gone. I leaned in and whispered, "She's using you." I couldn't help it. The words tumbled out.

"No," he said in a soft voice, putting his good hand on my arm. "God is using me."

We waited for the radiator to cool, and the preacher showed me how to add water, then we all climbed back into the truck. My mother drove, the preacher squished in the middle of the seat in the cab. At least she was helpful for once.

It was late afternoon when we'd crossed the California border. I expected us to whoop and holler, but nobody said a word. Everyone was all clammed up with their own thoughts. Even Sarah sensed the tension and stayed quiet.

Nobody talked at supper, either, but the preacher'd kept a polite smile on his face while we ate at the coffee shop inside the Mt. Shasta City Motel where we finally stopped. We'd had corned beef hash and homemade bread. It wasn't the supper I'd imagined, but it was better than potatoes and beans. An enormous, snowcapped mountain loomed over the town, visible through the windows, the last of daylight casting a pink glow on the snow. But nobody even commented on the beauty of the scene, as if jagged peaks rising out of nowhere were an everyday occurrence.

My mother had her bath. She'd used up most of the hot

water so when it was our turn, Jessie and I soaked in luke-warm water. But it felt good to be clean. I saved the paper-wrapped bar of motel soap to take with us. I washed Jessie's hair with Breck shampoo, making little peaks with the suds. Showed Jessie in the mirror how silly she looked. Her hair was getting long and each curl was a spring that bounced back when I pulled. Her giggles made me feel a little better.

Jessie perched on the edge of the bathtub to watch while I shampooed my hair. It didn't matter if Jessie saw me naked. She was my sister. It was my mother I hid from. Anything to avoid another lecture about the curse.

Bending backward under the bathtub faucet hurt my neck. My hair was so long and tangled it took forever to rinse. Just like my mother's hair. I didn't want to look like her. I didn't want to act like her, either. The water was gray when I got out. It swirled down the drain carrying little bits and pieces of fuzz and leaves and dirt out to the Pacific Ocean, where we were headed. It seemed wasteful and sad, all that water draining out of the tub.

"Vira sad?" Jessie'd asked.

I dried off and pulled on flannel pajamas, soft and worn with one button missing, but still clean since I'd been sleeping in T-shirts every night. I rubbed Jessie's hair with a rough motel towel. "Vira's okay," I'd lied.

"Vira misses Ray," she'd said. "Vira will see soon."

I was used to Jessie by then. Her words didn't scare me anymore. I accepted she was right and I'd see soon. My stomach jumped with joy and excitement and a little fear at seeing my father again. I thought about the German lady saying Jessie's leading me. Remembered I'd vowed to do what Jessie said. Go where she said to go.

So I told her about him.

I told her about my father's guitar and the songs he'd strummed for me, how he'd looked and smelled and laughed. "He loves thunderstorms," I said. "Rain always reminds me of him." Words spilled out. It was a relief talking about my father. Some of my memories had faded. Talking brought them back. I told Jessie about our secret rock back home where we spent so much time.

"Wait," I'd said. "Be right back." I opened the bathroom door a crack. My mother was sleeping. Grandma was silent in the other bed, facing the wall. My box was in a corner by my cot and quickly I dug in the pocket of my father's parka and pulled out the sock of treasures.

We sat on the battered tile and leaned against the bathroom wall, Jessie cuddling into my side. "This is my best one," I said, handing her the agate. "See how smooth it is? Look at the white swirls and the black dots. Ray said the dots are called dendrites."

"The pinecone's my favorite," said Jessie, holding it in the palm of her hand. "Like a Christmas tree pinecone. Only small."

"Yes. I always wanted to string some. Make a garland and decorate a tiny tree. Maybe they have these in California and we can decorate a Mabel-sized Christmas tree."

Jessie squealed. "Mabel would love that."

"Ray was a good father," I said, and I felt a catch in my throat. "You're so much alike. You have his green eyes, you know."

"I know," she said.

I talked a while longer even though Jessie's eyelids were beginning to droop. I left out the drinking parts. Didn't mention he never kept a job for more than a few weeks and disappeared for days on end, or how empty the house felt the times he never came home, and how the loneliness settled in the pit of my stomach like a dead thing, dragging me down. There was no good reason to tell her about his bruises from fights. Or the hundred times my mother poured whiskey down the sink and how often he stayed in bed, too sick or tired from drinking to move. Memories I'd tried hard to forget.

But talking about him brought those back too. He wouldn't be like that now. I squeezed my eyes shut. Pictured his face, listened for his voice. Heard instead the arguments and my mother's crying and the clink of the last few quarters in the savings jar.

I didn't tell Jessie that maybe he wasn't the husband our mother had wished for.

She didn't need to know all that.

I gave her every good memory I had. But then she said a strange thing.

"Ray's waiting for me," she'd said in a solemn little voice.

"What do you mean?" I'd asked.

"Waiting. He's waiting until I come."

"But Jessie, we're all going with you. He'll be there for all of us. Don't be scared."

"Not scared," she'd said. "He's waiting for me."

I let it go. "Yes, he's waiting for you," I'd said, even though suddenly my blood simmered with jealousy. It was me he'd loved. He was waiting for me. But that was mean. Jessie was my seventh treasure. I took a deep breath. Let her think what she wanted.

I was playing that day over in my mind — the dream,

that bath and conversation with Jessie, sitting in the dump of a motel room — when I felt another twang of pain in my back and wetness between my legs. I got up to go to the bathroom. I didn't turn on the light for fear of waking everyone. But the vacancy sign flashed blue in there too, just enough light to see the stain on my underwear. It was the curse. All that time had passed, me going on fifteen, and it had to be that night in that motel.

My mother's cosmetics bag was on the counter by the sink. I took out her belt and a sanitary napkin, fumbled with the clips. Got myself cleaned up. I wasn't scared or worried. I felt different though. Older. It was as if I'd be able to speak my mind from then on, now that my body was a woman's body and even though I knew that was a strange way to feel, the thought stuck. But I was not about to tell my mother. I'd never hear the end of it.

With new feelings surging through me, I rummaged through my mother's cosmetics bag. Pond's Cold Cream. Red nail polish. A tube of lipstick. Her hairbrush full of strands sticking out every which way.

I saw her hair scissors. Reached in and pulled the scissors out. Held them up in front of the mirror. Blue light glinted off the blades.

My father wasn't the husband my mother had needed. I couldn't shake that notion. She'd poured grease on his head that day. He ran away. But she didn't stop him, either. Why not?

I held my braid in one hand, felt the weight of it, the thick, dark hair woven in and out, dragging long and heavy on my neck every day for years and years. I didn't want to look like my mother anymore.

I raised the scissors and hacked that braid off.

As my hair fell to the floor, it occurred to me that my father didn't stop himself. He knew I loved him and he left anyway.

Chapter 24

E ureka wasn't much of a town. It looked a lot like Portage and even had a main street named Main Street. Same types of stores downtown, brick and stone buildings with display windows and striped awnings, only more ramshackle, not as cheerful as the buildings in Portage. I noticed a diner like Daisy's back home but the windows were smudged. A meat loaf with mashed potatoes ad was so faded it made the idea of eating there disgusting.

The air in Eureka smelled different than Portage air. That surprised me. It was fresh and a little fishy and filled with the scent of unfamiliar plants. Like wet grass up close. Downtown Portage was so near the canal that it always smelled marshy, like damp earth and algae. This smell was better.

A dress shop had a mannequin in the window wearing the latest ladies' suit style, according to the sign at the mannequin's feet, with a shortened peplum and narrower hemline. Where did ladies in Eureka wear those fashionable suits? But I saw my mother looking at it longingly as we pulled slowly down the street. Maybe it was enough just to own one. Grandma could probably make an exact copy. It might be fun to make a suit like that. Pick the right fabric, something that accentuated the waist. Notions like wooden buttons on the jacket and satin ribbon trim on the cuffs of the sleeves.

Next was a barber shop with a red-striped pole out front, a bank, and Smith Hardware, which apparently doubled as a fishing supply since the lettering on the window advertised tackle, bait, and minnows right next to a sign for three-penny nails.

They had a movie theater and the marquee read, "Now Playing: *The Bachelor and the Bobby-Soxer*, starring Cary Grant, Myrna Loy, and Shirley Temple." I hated Shirley Temple. She was too cute. Sickly sweet. I'd seen one of her dumb tap-dancing films once. My father took me against my mother's protests about wasting money on frivolities. I wished through the whole film Shirley Temple would trip and fall up there on that big screen.

A pretty, white church with a steeple was at one end of Main Street. An arched, stained-glass window glowed above the double doors. I glanced through the cab window to see if the preacher noticed the church. He was driving again, looking straight ahead with both hands on the wheel, his bandage unraveling a bit. I'd have to fix it later. It was hard to tell if he slowed to take a look at the church. The truck was already edging down the street an inch an hour.

At the other end of Main, I saw the county library, an elegant brick building with white columns and stone steps. Thick lawn in front, the kind of lawn for bare feet. Maybe I'd make friends with the librarian and she'd recommend books like Mrs. Keller always did. I still hadn't finished the first chapter of *A Tree Grows in Brooklyn*. But Francie and her Tree of Heaven were nagging at me so I knew I'd read it soon even if it meant there would be nothing left to look forward to. I'd write Mrs. Keller a letter and tell her how much I loved it. And then I'd read it again.

The preacher turned onto First Street. There was a grocery store called Steinberg's Market in the middle of the block. Wooden bins out front held colorful displays of lettuce and corn and red potatoes, with a pyramid of apples and another of peaches that looked juicy and fresh. I was surprised to see peaches so early in the season.

A tin Royal Crown Cola sign in the market's window made me thirsty just looking at it. The weather was warm. A summer day in full swing. I used thirst as my excuse for needing to stop.

We were going so slow I leaned over the side of the truck bed and stuck my face near the passenger window. It startled Grandma. She rolled down the window and swatted toward me as if I were a pesky fly. When I dodged, I noticed how light my head felt without my braid. I wasn't used to it. But I was glad the braid was gone. Even though my mother'd screamed when she saw me. "What have you done?" she'd said. The look of horror on her face was worth it.

"We're thirsty," I shouted, drawing Jessie into my bargain. I nodded so she'd get my meaning.

"We're thirsty," Jessie echoed.

"And Sarah needs water."

Sarah was panting. She did look hot, but that wasn't why I wanted to stop. The real reason was I needed sanitary napkins. I figured I was going to have to steal some. Steinberg's Market was as good a place as any.

The preacher pulled into a diagonal spot in front of the market. We all got out, stretching stiff legs. I looked up and down the street, half expecting my father to run right up and greet us. People strolled in and out of stores, going about their business, but no one looked familiar. I didn't see any yellow houses like I'd pictured.

The preacher wiped sweat off the back of his neck with a white handkerchief. I thought of the German lady's hanky in the pocket of my father's parka. The preacher's handkerchief reminded me of her words and warnings. A white hanky means truth. Was I close to the truth now? Was my father nearby?

White birds I'd never seen before swooped and spiraled, stabbing the air with long beaks and calling a strange, lonely cry. I patted my leg and Sarah jumped down. She was so happy to be out of that truck she did a whole-body wag. She stopped wagging and frowned at me when I tied her with a slip of rope to a post in front of Steinberg's. I rubbed her ears for a minute to apologize.

"Can Jessie and I get a Royal Crown?" I asked my mother. I knew we didn't have much money but I figured it was worth the risk to ask. Nothing tasted good like an ice-cold Royal Crown.

"You can get one bottle. We'll all share it," said my mother. She handed me fifty cents. "There'd better be change."

Like I could get a bus ticket out of there with the left-over pennies. My mother was still mad about me cutting my hair. She'd been using every little thing to make sure I knew it. I didn't care. I liked my hair short. Besides, I didn't want to press my luck. Even sharing a Royal Crown was better than nothing. It had been so long since we'd had anything sweet.

"C'mon, Jessie," I said and grabbed her hand.

The market was as clean and bright inside as it looked from the street. Wide plank floors were scrubbed to a high shine. The whole place smelled of lemon polish. A glass-front butcher's counter had a friendly looking old man wearing a white apron behind it. He was slicing roast beef on a cutting board and he smiled at us as we passed.

"Can I help you ladies?" he asked.

"No, thanks, we're fine." I dragged Jessie out of view.

I found the sanitary napkins in the remedies aisle next to the cough medicines and headache pills and all the other products for sick people. That was strange. Even though I called it the curse I didn't really think of it that way. Like it was something horrible. It seemed more of a bother than anything else. It made no sense the ladies' hygiene items were parked on shelves next to the remedies for ailments like the curse was a problem to be cured. Someday, I'd tell Jessie that it was nothing to worry about, but right now I had bigger problems.

I didn't want Jessie to see me steal.

I'd been teaching her to count. She was up to twenty-five and even though she usually forgot the numbers seven and twelve, she liked to count. It held her attention for long stretches of time. I pointed to the Johnson's Baby Aspirin and said, "Jessie, see how many bottles are on that shelf. Bet there are more than twenty-five." I figured that would give me enough time to stuff a travel-size box of sanitary napkins down the front of my overalls, which I hoped were baggy enough to hide it.

That's when I saw the boy. He was pushing a flat cart stacked high with boxes. He passed at the end of our aisle, whistling a tune I recognized but couldn't quite place. The boy didn't look our way but my heart pounded from the fear of getting caught.

I felt a tug on my overalls. Jessie pointed down the empty aisle.

"Saul," she said.

"What? What's sol?"

"Saul. That boy. Saul," she said again. Scurried behind me and shoved. Hard. "Go. Hurry."

"What are you talking about, Jessie?"

"Go," she said and pushed me again. Her eyes were glassy but she had that Kewpie-doll, impish smile I'd seen before.

I felt light-headed suddenly, and my spine tingled like when you read a creepy passage in a book you've been forbidden to read. Scary but delicious.

I took a step and as I did the boy rounded the corner, still whistling. Pushing his cart right toward us. He was beautiful. About sixteen. Tall and slender with a wild crop of curly brown hair. He seemed familiar, as if I'd met him before, but I knew that was impossible. I felt stupid for thinking it.

"Hi," he said in a voice changed to deep already. "Need some help?"

He had the longest and darkest eyelashes I'd ever seen. My voice stuck in my throat, and I burned with the knowledge of sanitary napkins in the front of my overalls. I crossed my arms over my chest. But I felt a stirring in my stomach and shivers up my spine. A feeling I'd never felt before.

"No," I squeaked out. "We're just looking around."

My heart pounded. What was wrong with me? I knew how bad I must look. Filthy and smelly as if I'd just finished slopping pigs in my baggy overalls, my face covered in freckles like flecks of dirt in need of scrubbing. Short hair whipped around by the wind in the back of the truck, now sticking up every which way. Suddenly I wished for my braid back. I was sure I looked like a boy as my mother'd said when she first saw my haircut. And the only thing making my chest stick out was the box of napkins. I still only had mosquito bites.

"I'm Saul Steinberg. This is my grandfather's store. Is that your dog out there?" he asked.

I nodded.

"What's your dog's name?"

Jessie piped up, hopping on one foot and back to her annoying self, the glassy-eyed look gone. "Her name's Sarah. We found her but she's ours now. This is Vira. She's my sister. She's pretty, isn't she?"

I could've swatted her. I gave her a dirty look to shush her and wished I could slip through the floor. But Saul laughed. A full belly laugh like he'd never been embarrassed his whole life and standing around talking to grubby girls was his favorite pastime. He seemed so sure of himself. Was that because he was older or because he was a boy and things are easier for boys?

"Yes, she is pretty," he said to Jessie. "I've never seen you two in here before and I work every afternoon during the summer. Just passing through?"

He was talking to Jessie but he stared at me. I wanted to blurt out our whole story, how we'd come all the way from Portage to find my father because my sister was a seer and she'd told us to. I wanted to tell him about the preacher and my mother and Grandma. How everything was all complicated and confusing and some days I was so mixed up I didn't know what to think. I wanted to say all that and somehow, I had the feeling he might understand. Maybe he'd tell me the one thing that would make sense to my mind.

"Do you have Royal Crown Cola?" I said instead.

"Sure. I'll show you," he answered.

We followed Saul to a cold case at the back of the store. Watched him pull out two icy bottles.

"No, we just want one," I said.

"I'll join you," he said.

"We need to go," I said. "My mother's waiting and she doesn't have a lot of patience."

I didn't want him to see us all sharing one bottle of Royal Crown. That would prove we were dirt poor. Not that he couldn't figure that out for himself by looking out the window at the preacher's dented truck, piled high with junk coated with dust. Scruffy people in grimy clothes leaning against it.

He did look.

"That your dad out there?" he asked.

I laughed. I couldn't help it. The thought of the preacher as my father struck my funny bone. Especially since he was in love with my mother. But I stopped mid-laugh. It really wasn't funny. Having the preacher for a father wouldn't be the worst thing that ever happened. He was kind and patient. The preacher made me think about God in new and different ways. A God who whispers, one who would hold your hand like a friend.

I tried to cover up my laughing by clearing my throat and started to answer but Jessie interrupted.

"No," she said, smiling her little white shell-toothed smile. "Our father's Ray. He's waiting for me."

I was horrified. My stomach flipped. I knew exactly how my mother'd felt when Jessie'd done the same thing to her — given away her secret. I grabbed Jessie's hand and squeezed to stop her talking.

"Ray?" asked Saul. He popped the caps off the drinks with the opener attached to the side of the cold case. A swirl of steam escaped from each bottle. He handed one to me. "Don't think I know a Ray. Thought I knew everyone around here."

"I'm sure you don't know him," I stammered. "He lives in a little yellow house way out of town." He knew I was lying. I could tell he guessed I didn't really know where my father's house was. I felt awful deceiving him with the lie and the stealing but at the same time I wondered why I even cared, having just met him. "We have to go. How much do I owe you?"

"On the house," he said.

Saul smiled. Clinked his bottle to mine.

"What's the hold up? We could've driven all the way back to Portage in the time it takes you to get one soda, Elvira. Move a little slower, why don't you?"

Grandma had snuck up as usual. But that time I was glad. I was in such a hurry to get out of there I almost hugged her. The box of napkins was slipping to my waist. I pushed Jessie toward the door and called thanks to Saul over my shoulder. Jessie fluttered her fingers in a wave. Grandma disappeared down an aisle.

But Saul followed us out.

He leaned against the wall, watching me. Sarah strained as I untied her, wagging as if I'd been gone forever. But the second she was loose, she beelined for Saul. Jumped him in a dog greeting, licking his face. Almost knocked him over. Saul rubbed Sarah's ears with both hands and laughed. I used the commotion to slip the sanitary napkins behind a pyramid of peaches. I couldn't steal from Saul Steinberg. He was too nice.

Saul stayed there, leaning on the wall of the market, arms folded. Watched as we pulled away from the curb.

"*Blueberry Hill!*" I blurted, leaning over the edge of the preacher's truck. My heart pounded with the beat of that song. "The tune you were whistling. It's 'Blueberry Hill.'" How could I have forgotten that song?

Saul took a few steps forward, stepped into the street, cupped his hands around his mouth. "By Glenn Miller," he called. "My favorite. See you when I see you."

Jessie giggled.

§

I thought about Saul on the short drive to the beach where we'd camp for the night. I thought about him when I saw the Pacific Ocean for the first time — transparent blue-green waves crashing on black rocks sending shimmering spray skyward. The sound was so powerful, like wind through trees or summer storms, loud and pounding, the rhythm soothing and scary at the same time.

I thought of Saul when I felt, for the very first time, hot sand on bare feet and I dug down with my toes to cool and wet. I'd never cared about boys before. What was wrong with me? But he stayed in my mind while I helped build the fire and laid out blankets and ate supper. "Blueberry Hill" stuck with me too. Like it used to when my father whistled it.

The preacher and Jessie dug in the sand at the water's edge, and my mother sat by herself on a driftwood log a ways off, staring at the waves. I was still humming "Blueberry Hill" and thinking about Saul when Grandma snuck up and shoved a grocery sack in my hands.

I looked inside. It was a big box of sanitary napkins.

"How did you know?" I asked.

She snorted. "Women's intuition," she said. "Any trouble? Any pains?"

I shook my head. "Not really."

"Good. You take after me, not your mother. Although, I suppose it's not her fault, the way she is."

I couldn't decide if it was a good thing or a bad thing to take after Grandma. I supposed when it came to the curse, taking after Grandma was better than suffering my mother's complaints. "Thanks," I said, grateful for the favor.

I thought about all the arguments Grandma'd had with my mother. All the hurtful things she'd said and done. They were so different and, at the same time, so very much alike.

But for the first time since I could remember, Grandma hadn't criticized my mother. She'd said something good.

She'd said it wasn't my mother's fault the way she was. Even if she was only talking about the curse. Suddenly, that made me angry. I couldn't stop my thoughts from rushing forward.

"Maybe a lot of other things aren't her fault, either," I said. "Maybe she can't help the way she is because of you. Maybe she just needs a little kindness from you once in a while."

My stomach lurched. Why was I sticking up for my mother now? I never talked back to Grandma like that. I waited for her to explode. Walk away in a huff, throwing spiteful remarks at me over her shoulder like she always did. Instead, she folded her arms and stepped closer. I saw her eyes shine with tears, though none fell.

"Like you need a little kindness from her?" she said, her chin inches from mine. Her face crumpled, the lines around her mouth sagged. She looked worn out. "She made the same mistakes I did, Elvira. Married too young. Married someone who couldn't hold a job, same as my husband. I knew she'd have trouble with Ray. I recognized the pattern. Saw it in my own life. But it never mattered. Nothing a wife says will matter if the husband doesn't listen."

I remembered what the German lady had said when she'd tried to warn her husband before they got on the boat. He hadn't listened. I knew what Grandma said was the truth. Some things you could not change. But it still made me angry.

"Why did you make her wedding dress, then? If you hated my father so much?"

"I didn't hate him, Elvira. And I loved her. Connie was my life. I raised her alone. She was all I had. But I couldn't have stopped her from marrying Ray. Her mind was made up. She was lovely in that dress. I thought a beautiful start might give her a chance to be happy, and she *was* happy for a while. But Ray never held a job. He drank. Disappeared. Brawled like a bulldog."

"Why didn't you do something?"

"I tried. But she wouldn't listen. She's stubborn as a mule. I tried to tell her that I made the same mistakes my mother did and she was following in our footsteps. It's a pattern, Elvira. When you came along, things were hard. I watched her repeat everything I did wrong. She's just like me, and you are like her."

I shook my head. I wasn't like either of them.

"I saw you talking to that boy. Don't make the same mistakes, Elvira. The apple doesn't fall far from the tree. It's up to you to break the pattern. It's why I came along on this fool trip in the first place. I want to *see* you break it."

She did walk away then. I'd never heard Grandma say she loved my mother. Maybe that was the closest Grandma would ever get to an apology for all her years of criticizing. At least I knew why now. She'd done the best she could. My mother had repeated Grandma's life with all its worry and fear and unsteadiness. In one way, Grandma was right. The apple didn't fall far from the tree. I'd never heard my mother say she loved me, either.

But that didn't mean she didn't. Maybe my mother had a hard time saying the words, like Grandma did. My mother had crossed the country to find my father. Somewhere, deep down, she had truly loved him. He never should have left her. We were so close to finding him. Would he be the husband my mother wanted? Or would he still be the same one Grandma criticized?

My mother criticized me. Maybe criticizing all the time covered up the pain of their failures. I *would* break the pattern. I loved my father, but I would never marry someone who drank. It hurt too much.

A single star clung to the sky as dusk settled over the beach. I pictured the star as God's home. "Ask a question," the preacher had said. "Ask for a clear path to the answer."

I prayed for the first time. *Will I break the pattern? God, please send a clear path to the answer.*

As I prayed, it was the preacher I pictured. I trusted him. He'd shown me how to believe in God. I didn't understand everything God intended, but neither did the preacher and he still had faith. I realized then what I had to change if I didn't want to be like my mother or Grandma. I had to be myself. Not another apple off the same old tree. Maybe that's what God had in mind for me anyway. He wanted me to just be me.

I'd start by giving all the love and kindness I had to give.

Chapter 25

It wasn't daylight, exactly, when I opened my eyes and looked through the screened window of the tent. It was the final lingering moment before dawn when the world is silent and still, and the sky is the murky gray of dirty dishwater. I could almost feel that color. A gloomy mood settled on me that matched.

The air was damp and chilly. Gritty sand was on my face and in my teeth. A wind whipped the tent and carried the smell of fish right through the canvas. I quietly pulled on clothes and dug in my box for my father's parka.

Jessie's eyes fluttered and opened. I put my finger to my lips. She wriggled out from under her pile of blankets.

I shook my head. I wanted some time to myself.

She nodded. Held Mabel up and made her nod too.

I shook my head again and she frowned and stuck out her bottom lip so I gave up. Grabbed her sweater and shoes and gestured for her to follow me as I undid the zipper on the tent flaps.

A wet mist hung low over the beach as far as I could see in both directions. The ocean rose and fell, the waves slapping rocks in steady rhythm like soldiers' boots, only the sound made me feel sad and heavy that morning instead of excited like it had last night when I was thinking about Saul.

I had the feeling I'd see Saul again. I had the feeling we had more to say.

I zipped my father's parka. Checked for my treasures in one pocket and the German lady's hanky in the other.

"Put your sweater on, Jessie. It's cold," I whispered. Why was I whispering? We were far enough away from the tents so no one could hear. I set Mabel on a rock. Helped Jessie as she struggled with her sleeves. It didn't feel like June. It felt like the middle of winter.

Jessie put both hands on my head for balance as I knelt to pull on her shoes and lace them tight.

"Vira sad?" she asked.

"I don't know. Maybe."

"See Ray today. He's waiting for me."

Suddenly I felt exasperated, fed up. Sick of it all. The whole idea seemed so wasteful and stupid, thinking my father was waiting here for us after all that time. At that moment I couldn't imagine how I'd ever believed my father was still alive. No matter how much I wished I could see him again, the idea of my father waiting struck me hard as silly. Childish. Like wishing on a star or throwing salt over your shoulder. I felt a powerful rage welling up. I took it out on Jessie.

"Where is he waiting, Jessie? Do you really believe he's here somewhere? Tell me where. Take me to him if you know everything and see so much. You don't even know him. I'm the one he loved. You weren't even born. He never loved you."

I felt horrible the second the words were out of my mouth. A day hadn't even passed since I'd resolved to show love and kindness and there I was acting hurtful and mean. I sounded exactly like Grandma and my mother — critical, judging, careless with words. I would never break the pattern that way.

Jessie grabbed Mabel. Turned and ran.

She was a tiny speck down the beach before I came to my senses and ran after her. It was hard to run in sand. My feet felt heavy and clumsy. I was so slow. I heard Sarah barking from the back of the preacher's truck where she was tied. Everyone would wake up to that barking.

The wind was fierce, whipping my hair and the surf. Even gulls struggled against the force of it, screaming. I wanted to scream too. Jessie was way ahead. Then gone, hidden by an outcropping of jagged rocks. No. There she was. I had to catch up. Even as I ran, my heart pounding in my chest and sand stinging my eyes, I looked down and saw all the little, white shells scattered on the beach. The perfect, white shells I'd always wanted for a necklace. One for me, one for Jessie. I promised myself when I caught up with Jessie, I'd say sorry, I didn't mean it. It's just a gloomy mood. I'd hug her close and smooth her shiny curls and we'd collect as many shells as our pockets would hold. We'd string them until we had two beautiful necklaces to keep forever.

But I lost sight of her.

One split second in the gray fog and she disappeared. I screamed her name. The wind took my voice to the waves.

I saw the sign. It was rusted and bent, battered by weather and bullet holes. It warned "No Swimming. Rip Tide." I didn't know what a rip tide was but I knew it was something bad.

I ran harder. My knees throbbed and my chest hurt. I glimpsed Jessie on the beach right at the edge of the ocean, still running, her feet kicking up froth and sand.

"Jessie," I screamed.

She didn't turn. But I was catching up. I was closer.

"Jessie," I screamed again. "Stop!"

A wave took her.

In one motion, one swell like an open, hungry mouth, the sea swallowed Jessie and carried her out. Her head bobbed twice and she was gone.

Mabel lay face down in the sand, waves licking her feet. I tossed her aside and dove. The water was freezing. It took my breath away as I splashed and flailed and tried to swim to the place I'd seen Jessie's head bobbing on the waves.

A huge swell knocked me back. Water went up my nose and I tasted salt.

I went under.

It was cold and dark and a rushing sound filled my ears. The ocean shoved me back and forth.

My father's parka was weighing me down. It was so heavy I could hardly move my arms.

I couldn't see Jessie. Couldn't find her. *Where are you? Where?*

It got darker and the water dragged me down to where

it was black and frightening and I thought I would die. Suddenly, I saw an orange flash and everything calmed, as though my struggle was over. I floated in the silence. Looked up and saw my father waving from a ledge. Smiling. Waving at me. He stood in orange light the color of flames. But blinding white light surrounded his head and shoulders. Pulsing, breathing, moving. As though the white light had a heartbeat. My father waved. I felt my old anger from the dream. Why didn't he save me?

But then I understood.

He wasn't waving to me.

He wasn't waving to me and he wasn't there to save me.

He was waving hello. To Jessie.

He was dead and he was welcoming her. He'd been waiting for her.

My dream had been telling me all along what to expect, what was to come. But I'd never seen the white light in my dream.

My father wasn't waiting for me.

Hope slid out of my body. All the hope I'd made myself feel washed out in a rush, gulped down by the ocean like a single teardrop, leaving me empty and weak. All the wishes blurred and faded. I'd never see my father again. I'd believed for nothing. Why would God do this to me?

I could let the water take me. Float in the silence until my last breath exploded in my chest and my lungs filled, the water dragging me down to the dark. Then I'd be with my father too. Like Jessie, I'd be with him forever.

I stopped struggling. My arms and legs swayed with the swells. I was weightless. Drained. A dead fish in the ocean.

The orange light flashed. I was too close. It was drawing me to it. And then I heard my father's voice.

"Race!"

It was loud in my head, echoing, like a speaker at the movies high above the balcony seats. My heart fluttered. The white light around my father's head glimmered brighter. Blinding. I wanted to close my eyes to it.

No. Take me with you. Please. I didn't want to race. I was too tired. Why was he telling me this? Rage took over my body, coursed through me. It wasn't fair. I wanted to scream at my father's voice. I wanted to say, *No, don't leave me. I'll be good and I won't talk back and I'll help Mama every day.*

But then I knew what he meant. He was already gone. Nothing would bring him back. I had to save myself.

But I couldn't live without Jessie.

I had to get air.

I was so tired. So weak. I clutched at the zipper on my father's parka. Yanked with all the strength I had left, kicking my feet and struggling to get my arms out.

Jessie shouldn't die. She didn't make my father leave. I did. It was my fault he was gone. If Jessie died, that would be my fault too. I *had* to save her. I needed her and she needed me. This was a race I had to win.

I wriggled free. As my father's parka started to sink I remembered my treasures. I grabbed. Missed. Tried again and clasped the edge of the pocket. The parka was so heavy. My arms ached. I lifted the pocket flap and reached in. It was the wrong pocket. The German lady's hanky floated into my hand as I lost my grip on the parka and it sank, the weight of my treasures dragging it down.

A white hanky means truth. I knew the truth now. My father was dead. My mother could let him go. I could let him go. I remembered the story the German lady told me. She still lived with the guilt of death. "I never forgive myself," she'd said. I'd never forgiven myself for making my father leave, and like the German lady, I'd carried that guilt all this time.

At once, I felt calm, peaceful, like the ocean filled with love, wrapping me in the comfort of strong, capable arms. I wasn't alone. I felt cared for. Loved. Was God holding my hand? Was he whispering, like a friend?

Suddenly, the water lifted me, up and up, the surface visible, lighter and lighter blue. I broke through, gasping, exhausted. Wheezing, choking. Treading water with numb limbs but breathing cold, clear air.

I could see the beach. If I swam hard, I could get there.

But the German lady had said something else.

"Sometimes cannot change what is to happen. Sometimes can," she'd said.

I could change this.

I drew a deep breath. Dove back to where it was dark and frightening. Kicked with new strength, pumping hard with my arms.

And my hand touched something.

Something soft and giving.

Something tangled.

A wave knocked me back. I kicked harder, faster, stronger, forcing my body downward.

My hand touched something again.

I stared through the murky, bottomless water, my eyes stinging, lungs bursting, head pounding.

insight

I reached down and yanked those curls and hauled us both up. The radiant white light burst upon the water, revealing the way.

Chapter 26

I lay on the wet sand at the edge of the water and hugged Jessie close, trying to warm her, both of us shaking from the fear and the cold. She'd coughed up a lot of water when I thumped her back, and her lips and fingers were eerily blue.

The sun had burst through the fog but it was still early morning. The wind was calmer now. I carried Jessie to a crevice in a clump of rocks where we'd be sheltered, away from the waves. Scooted her back and plodded with shaking knees the few feet to pick up Mabel. She was exactly where I'd tossed her. I was amazed the ocean hadn't thrown us miles down the beach. It felt like we'd been under so long. I shuddered. Had we really almost died? It was hard to believe. But here we were, wet and coughing, freezing and exhausted. Alive. Both of us.

"Ray's gone," whispered Jessie, her eyes closed and her voice hoarse.

"I know," I whispered back. "But you're here."

I smoothed Jessie's matted curls. Gathered her small body close to my chest. She coughed again and I rubbed her back. Feeling was slowly returning to my numb fingers.

"Ray called for a long time. He was waiting for me."

"I know."

"The white light wanted him. He kept calling me. Waiting."

I'd seen the orange light in my dream a hundred times. But not the blinding white light. When I dragged Jessie to the surface, the white light illuminated the ocean like a searchlight probes the sky. Pulsing, beating, like a living thing. I'd felt peace beneath the water. I knew, with all my heart, the truth of the white light. Jessie had led us to the truth and the truth was God.

"Ray's in the white light now. He's with God," I said. "God will take care of him."

And I would take care of Jessie. I needed her. My father's love was inside my heart. I would pass it on. I missed him, but I could finally say good-bye. At the little girl's funeral the preacher said, "With God, there is always joy." It felt good to think maybe my father was happy.

"Ray was waiting because he had to tell me something, Vira."

"What? What did he tell you?"

"He said, 'Put the guilt aside.' He said, 'Take it from me; nobody can carry a burden that big.' What's a burden, Vira?"

"It's a big, heavy weight of thinking you did something wrong," I said. "Can you hear him right now?"

Jessie shook her head, wet curls dripping on her cheeks. With my thumb, I gently wiped the drips away. I would put my burden down. Forgive myself. It seemed a lot of work coming all this way for that one reason, but my father was right. Nobody can carry a burden that big. The German lady couldn't. I couldn't. It hurt too much.

"He won't call me anymore," said Jessie. "He's gone for good now. It's not Ray on the porch, Vira."

"What?" I could barely talk my throat hurt so much from screaming and saltwater and tears trying to get out. My arms and legs throbbed and my ears had a steady, high-pitched ring that wouldn't fade.

"The yellow house. It's not Ray on the porch of the yellow house. The one you see in your mind."

"How did you —?" But even as I asked it I knew how Jessie knew. Like she saw other things, like God gave her the words when the words needed saying. She knew like she always would know. Seeing was a part of who Jessie was.

"Who is it then?" I asked.

Jessie looked up at me. Her green eyes were clear. Color was coming back to her face and lips. She was weak now but she'd be fine. She'd grow up strong and I'd be there to love her. She snuggled closer.

"Everybody has a little bit of seeing, Vira. You already know some of it," she said, curling her fingers around my hand. "You have to listen inside. Picture the yellow house. I will help you."

Everybody has a little bit of seeing. I closed my eyes. Tiny blue dots flitted and danced. At first I saw nothing, but soon colored shadows became hazy images. The edges sharpened, and I imagined it then, that little yellow house with the white picket fence. I saw red roses in bloom. In the distance, on a little hill, was a white church, its steeple reaching to puffy clouds and blue sky. Beyond, waves crashed on a beach and gulls circled.

I breathed deeply, felt the squeeze of Jessie's fingers, and saw a person sitting on the steps of the porch. As I watched, he stood up. Waved in greeting and moved toward me, walking unhurried down the front sidewalk, stepping lightly, and it was as though his heart was light too. His heart matched that step.

"It's Saul. Saul Steinberg, sitting on the steps of the yellow house," I whispered. "He's older, a little taller maybe, but it's him. How can that be?"

Jessie nodded. "Keep looking," she said, her green eyes glassy.

I closed my eyes again. Saw Saul move toward me and reach out a hand, flashing a smile that lit up his eyes, and the smile felt familiar, as though saved for me and me alone. My hair was long again but I wore it loose, and the ends curled from the moisture in the air. I tucked a stray strand behind my ear and took Saul's hand. We walked toward the yellow house.

Then my mother kicked the screen door open with her foot. The preacher was right behind her, carrying four white plates and forks. He stuck out his elbow to hold the door for my mother. She carried a white china platter. On it was Holiday Cake, white icing dribbling down the sides and pooling on the scalloped edges of a paper doily. I could almost taste the cranberries and walnuts. My mother set the cake on a table covered in a fringed blue cloth. The preacher placed his arm around my mother's waist and smiled as Saul and I joined them on the porch.

"Oh," I said, as I opened my eyes. "It's beautiful. Thank you for letting me see it. Do we really live there? The preacher too? And where are you? You're not in the picture." For a second, my heart pounded. But Jessie giggled.

"I'm playing with the new baby in the house. Don't tell them, Vira. You can't."

I thought about all the times Jessie had clammed up. How did she know when to stay silent? It would be a hard secret to keep. A new baby? My mother was forty-two. I chuckled at the look I could picture on Grandma's face when she heard that news. But somehow, I had the feeling the preacher would win Grandma over like he'd done with my mother and Jessie and me.

There was more to my life and in some way, Saul would be a part of it. Jessie had given me a picture that proved it. And I would always listen to Jessie.

&

I saw Sarah first. She broke through the fog at a dead run, her bark faint, then loud and sharp as she got closer, the soft parts of skin around her mouth jiggling as she ran. Sand scattering behind her in a wild spray. I watched Sarah come. Then I saw them behind Sarah — my mother, Grandma, and the preacher — running too. It seemed they ran so slow, as if in a dream, surrounded by the gray fog. So slow they'd never reach us.

Jessie smiled a tiny smile, then Sarah was there, barking and wagging, jumping all over us and kicking up sand. Licking my tears that finally fell. I picked up Jessie and she leaned her head on my shoulder. I saw them, still running, and it felt right that the preacher was with them. He was family. I knew the preacher would ease my mother's pain when I told her my father was really gone.

I slowly walked to meet them. Sarah circled me wildly and raced to the edge of the ocean, snapping at the froth on the waves that rolled in and out, in and out, faithful, permanent, constant, something to depend on like the moon rising or the sun setting or trust in true love.

I looked down and saw all the little shells.

I balanced Jessie on my hip and bent to pick up one. Its surface was shiny and slick, shimmering white with narrow brown stripes evenly spaced, perfect. I would gather a thousand shells. I'd make necklaces, one for Jessie, and one for me.

I'd make a necklace for my mother too.

I pulled the German lady's handkerchief from the pocket of my overalls, wrung the seawater out, and smoothed the edges of lace. Jessie told us the truth and led us here. Now it was time I told my mother the truth.

I wrapped that tiny shell inside and handed the handkerchief to my mother. She reached for it and our fingers brushed and held.

Chapter 27

I'd slept soundly all night, better than I had in a long time. The morning sun was warm on my back and the sea was calm. Maybe the ocean was sorry for causing me so much trouble. I climbed on a rock, away from the tents where everyone was just beginning to stir. I'd brought *A Tree Grows in Brooklyn* with me, the old picture of my mother and father marking where I'd left off. I wasn't afraid to read it anymore. I'd just begun chapter two, where Francie goes to the shabby little library that she feels is as beautiful as a church. Like Francie, I knew a library was a place of peace and comfort and companionship. Like church must be. As I read, I realized God had given me a lot to think about lately. Maybe he *had* watched over me on this journey, as Mrs. Keller had said. I'd hold *A Tree Grows in Brooklyn* in my heart right next to the memory of her.

For now, though, I put the book down on the rock. The rock was a good spot — my father would've liked it. He'd point out the fluffy clouds above. He'd notice the changes in the blue of the ocean, deep as night on the horizon and pale green, transparent, where the ocean rolled in shallow. He would've mentioned the sun reflecting, sparkling on the water in bright patterns like a fairy twirling and flitting in a magical dance across the surface. He'd given that gift of noticing to me.

I heard a low whine. Felt a wet nose nudging my hand. Sarah leaped for a pat, then she curled in the sand beside the rock, content nearby.

The cries of the gulls and the rhythm of the waves lulled me. I closed my eyes and leaned back. Like back home. Like my father and me on our secret rock. I listened to the sounds. Jessie was the only treasure I had left, but I had memories. I'd never forget.

I thought about last night's funeral.

It wasn't a real funeral but we'd said good-bye to my father. It was the preacher's idea. Jessie and I picked wild-flowers, orange poppies and purple vetch. We'd thrown them to the sea, watched as they'd floated in the setting sun and then scattered, becoming tiny dark dots carried out by the waves. The preacher'd said kind words and he'd read from the Bible. My mother cried a little but she'd brightened when I stood beside her. I told her that with God, there is always joy.

We'd all sung "Amazing Grace." Even Grandma sang.

It felt good to say good-bye. I had the preacher to thank for that. We'd never have thought of that on our own.

"Elvira? What are you doing?"

My mother's voice startled me. I sat up so fast it made me dizzy. Started to hide *A Tree Grows in Brooklyn* behind my back but then thought better of it. What did it matter, really, if my mother saw the book?

"Thinking," I said.

"I brought you a blanket," she said, our blue-and-yellow quilt draped across her arm.

"Thanks, but I'm not cold."

"Can I sit with you a minute? I want to talk to you."

I scooted over and my mother unfolded the quilt. Placed it on the rock, taking her time spreading it out, smoothing the wrinkles, brushing a few grains of sand. She glanced at my book and the customary scowl passed over her face, but it was gone in an instant, replaced by an expression I couldn't read. She climbed awkwardly and settled beside me. Her shoulder touched mine. She brought her knees up and yanked her dress. Rested her chin on her knees and clasped her hands around her legs. Cleared her throat.

"I want to tell you something I've never told anyone," she said in a shaky voice. "I never even told Grandma. It's about your father. And me. Something you probably don't even remember."

My heart pounded. My mother looked so scared. Like a little kid just awake after a nightmare. Big-eyed, pale, breathing fast and heavy.

"What?" I said. "What don't I remember?"

My mother reached in her pocket. Pulled out a yellowed piece of paper, folded in half and wrinkled like it had been wadded up once but smoothed out over and over again. She handed it to me. One tear trickled down her cheek.

I unfolded the paper.

I did remember.

It was my father's note. The note he'd left on the kitchen table for me when he'd enlisted.

My mother had kept it all this time.

My hands shook when I saw his careful printing. I could smell him. Hear his voice. See his face.

> *Good-bye Elvira,*
>
> *Be a good girl and help your mother. She loves you. I'll write when I'm on a ship and I'll see you soon. When I'm missing you, I'll be whistling "Blueberry Hill."*
>
> *— Dad*

I looked at that word, "Dad," and all the memories came flooding back. All my feelings of guilt for thinking I made him run away. All the years of missing him. My whole body went limp, and I put my head down and cried. But it wasn't a pain kind of crying. It was cleansing, healing. I felt like I could cry forever.

"I'm so, so sorry, Elvira," my mother said, her voice heavy with tears. "I didn't mean it. I never wanted him to die. I never would have told him to leave if I thought he'd die."

My stomach flipped. I choked. Sat there coughing, trying to get a deep breath. I looked up at her crumpled, sad face, tears streaking her cheeks, her chin trembling.

"What do you mean?" I whispered the question but it felt like a scream.

"Don't look at me like that, Elvira. You couldn't possibly blame me any more than I blame myself. All this time I've lived with the guilt. He woke me when he came back that night. He was drunk. I told him to leave and never come back. I killed him. It's my fault. When I believed we'd find him, I thought I'd get a second chance. I thought I could finally say I was sorry. He had his problems, Elvira, but I'd loved him for so long."

She sobbed then. Her guilt was bottomless. She cried and cried. I let her. I didn't stop her or pat her back or tell her I loved her. I was too shocked to move. My mind was numb. All this time I'd believed it was me who made my father leave. I'd felt awful every day of my life since he'd gone.

Until yesterday. "Nobody can carry a burden that big," he'd told Jessie. Until then, I'd believed my pain would never go away.

But my mother had asked him to leave. She carried the burden. Not me. My father's message was for her.

So I told my mother the truth. I told her everything about that day on the porch with my father. How I'd wanted to run away. Get away from her. I told her I'd hated her that day for pouring the grease on my father's head and for ruining my favorite dress. We both cried when I explained how, all this time, I thought I'd planted the idea of running away in my father's mind and how I didn't stop him from leaving when I'd had the opportunity.

I told her I knew how much guilt hurt.

"You have to forgive yourself," I said, and I put my hand on her arm, stroked it, something I'd never done before. She didn't pull away, and I thought maybe we could start over, try a little kindness once in a while. "Ray gave Jessie a message. He said, 'Put the guilt aside. Take it from me;

nobody can carry a burden that big.' He knew what guilt felt like too. I think he would've enlisted anyway because in his mind he was doing the right thing. He wanted to do something that would make us proud. But he would have come home if he could have."

"How do you know?"

"I know because he loved you," I said. "And if he would've come home, you would've let him back in like you always did before."

"Yes. I would have," she said, in a quiet voice. "You're right, Elvira."

"But that wasn't God's plan," I said.

"You sound like Don."

"I know." We were silent for a while, sitting side by side, leaning into each other. Thinking our own thoughts. Listening to each other's breathing. I picked up *A Tree Grows in Brooklyn* and slipped out the photograph of my mother and father. Handed it to her. I thought she would cry again but she smiled instead.

"Pretty dress," I said. "Grandma said it's long gone. At least there's a photograph of you wearing it on your wedding day."

She ran her thumb along the edge as if polishing silver. "No. It's not long gone. I still have the dress. I saved it for you." She placed the palm of her hand on my cheek, then removed it and smoothed the quilt instead as if that one gesture showed more than she was ready for. It didn't matter. I could wait.

Sarah jumped to the rock, put her nose right in my face to make sure I was all right. I *was* all right. I felt lighter than I ever had, cleaned out, refreshed. I rubbed Sarah's ears.

Buried my face in her fur. She smelled damp and musty but she smelled like my dog. I'd know that smell anywhere.

My mother sighed. A long, worn-out sound. "I really believed Ray was here. I truly thought Jessie was leading us to him."

I remembered what the preacher had said about denial and how it was the strangest state of mind. People believed what they wanted to believe, disregarding facts even if the facts were staring them in the face. Denial creates false hope. "But he *was* here," I said. "Jessie did see him. Just not in the way that we'd hoped. Jessie carried out God's plan. I don't understand it all but I think God wanted us to put the past behind us and start fresh."

"Maybe there is something to faith, Elvira, but it was still a long way to come for that lesson. The preacher — I mean Don — said he'd take us back. He said if that's what I wanted to do, he'd give us another ride. I guess we'll head out tomorrow morning."

"Back? Back to Portage?"

This had never occurred to me. I was not going back. I was staying here. The yellow house was here. Jessie led us here for a bigger purpose. The roar of the ocean matched the pounding in my head. I turned to glare at my mother.

But I felt suddenly calm. The flash of anger at my mother's words left me like a sparrow taking flight. I smiled at her instead. We would not go back. I knew.

"There's no reason to stay here now, Elvira. Ray's gone. As much as I wanted to believe he was waiting, he's not." She looked straight into my eyes, searching, and I thought for the first time in a long time my mother really noticed me. She was listening.

"You have a reason to stay," I said.

I pointed. The preacher was building a fire to start coffee and Jessie sat in the sand digging tunnels. Mabel was propped nearby. It made me happy to see Jessie pretending and playing like a normal little girl. Mabel's dress was filthy. I'd have to make her another one soon. The preacher joined Jessie and soon they were so absorbed in digging, they didn't notice a group of gulls creeping closer, looking for tidbits of food. I knew the preacher would shoo the squawking gulls. There was no one I trusted more with Jessie. And I trusted God. This was God's plan, like the preacher had said all along. We were meant to be a family. The preacher loved Jessie like I did. He loved all of us. Well, not Grandma. That could take some time.

I couldn't tell my mother everything that Jessie showed me. She probably wouldn't believe me anyway. But I had to convince her this was our new home.

"There," I said. "The preacher and Jessie and Grandma. Your reason to stay. Me. I'm your reason to stay. We're a family. Stay because the preacher needs a church of his own. He only wants a little church with a small congregation and comfortable pews. He needs a room at the church where he can hold Alcoholics Anonymous meetings to help people stop drinking. It's fine work. Stay so he can have that. Make us a family."

"How do you know these things?" My mother wiped her eyes with a corner of the quilt. Her face showed how much she wanted everything to be all right.

"Everything will be all right," I said, and I knew I sounded like Jessie. Reading minds. But it wasn't like that. It was God giving the words when the words needed saying.

She nodded. "I'll put some thought into it, Elvira. I'll talk to Don. He's a good man and he's been very patient with me. We'll see."

"Don loves you," I said. "He loves Jessie. And me."

"I know."

Sarah barked. Sat up, alert. Sniffed the air.

A group of boys tumbled down the sand dunes in the rough and wild way of boys. They kicked off shoes, rolled trouser legs, and began a game of football. One was taller than the others. He had dark, curly hair. He seemed to be the leader of the group. The boy took a few steps backward, raised his arm, and the football soared. Another caught it and landed in the sand, everyone piling on top of him.

Sarah whined. I remembered Jessie's small hands nudging me, pushing me at Steinberg's Market. Saul noticed me looking and gave a little wave. I waved back, not getting up. I put my hand on Sarah's head and could feel her quivering with pleasure.

"Wait," I said to her. "Not yet."

She wagged her tail, flicking sand. Looked at me with a question in her big brown eyes. I rubbed her ears and grabbed a handful of thick fur on the scruff of her neck.

Saul stepped away from the group of boys. Started walking toward me. The boys glanced my way, glanced at Saul, and continued with the football game.

I watched Saul come.

It felt like I'd watched him walk that beach a thousand times.

He started to whistle. I knew what the tune would be before it reached my ears. "Blueberry Hill." My father's favorite song. My favorite song.

"Now, Sarah. Go."

Sarah raced toward him, wagging as she ran, her tail and excitement throwing her whole gait off kilter. I laughed. I knew just how Sarah felt.

I kicked off my shoes and stepped down into the sand. I looked at my mother over my shoulder. "I have a reason to stay," I said, but I said it kindly, with as much love as I could put into my voice.

I walked slowly.

There was no need to hurry.

Someday I'd tell Saul the whole story.

For now, I needed a friend.

Talk It Up!

Want free books?
First looks at the best new fiction?
Awesome exclusive merchandise?

We want to hear from you!

Give us your opinions on titles, covers, and stories.
Join the Z Street Team.

Email us at zstreetteam@zondervan.com
to sign up today!

Also—Friend us on Facebook!

www.facebook.com/goodteenreads

- Video Trailers
- Connect with your favorite authors
- Sneak peeks at new releases
- Giveaways
- Fun discussions
- And much more!